TWINS

Lindsey Cole

CONTENTS

Prologue...6

1	Tyler and Ryan Godfrey	8
2	Their Birthday	12
3	Recollection	22
4	Dead or Alive	31
5	Mirror	40
6	Reunion	48
7	Ryan's Antagonist	54
8	Timeline of Cheats	65
9	Anxiety of the Knowing	75
10	The Art of Isolation	83
11	Run Away with the Runaway	90
12	The Keeper of the Keys	95
13	A System Leak	104
14	An Unlucky Gamble	111

Epilogue...119

Prologue
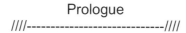

Two small children ran through the meadow behind their house happily playing a game of war with their fingers disguised as pistols, shooting at one another with grins on their faces. "Tyler! They're infiltrating our airships and bases! We must act quickly!" Ryan said, pointing to the sky with his index finger, gesturing to the make-believe airships.

 "Ryan, what's our plan of attack?" his older brother Tyler said, getting on one knee as to show a sign of loyalty. Ryan's face went blank as if his brain was filled with confusion.

"What's that mean?" he asked, looking a little embarrassed. Tyler shrugged, his brown hair falling into his eyes.

"... Maybe it means how we fight?"

Ryan shrugged but continued on with their game. "We shall take an emergency airship in order to ambush them!" Tyler nodded and started to initiate the startup sequence for the make-believe airship. "Hop on, Sir, we leave in ten seconds and counting!"

As Tyler started to count down, Ryan hopped onto the make-believe airship, but in the process he tripped on a discarded rock, falling onto his brother. The two chuckled and rolled on the grass, looking at the clouds. "Hey, Tyler?" the younger of the two whispered as if anything louder would ruin everything, "Why do Ma and Dad fight?"

Tyler lay next to Ryan with a serious expression on his face. "I don't think either of them is happy."

"Are they going to split up?" Ryan pouted. "What's going to happen to us if they do?"

"I don't like thinking of what could happen…" he said, his breath wavering.

The two of them were connected in a way normal siblings weren't. If they were separated, they'd break. Neither of them liked to think about that. Neither of them liked thinking about what it would be like if they woke up one day and they weren't greeted by the face the two of them shared. Just being… alone. Completely and utterly alone.

Things with Ma and Dad were quiet for a little while after that. They didn't know why at first, but then they walked into a building that said 'Family Court'. Each of them received a small stuffed bear from serious-looking adults wearing suits, and Ma and Dad went into a room while the two of them played in the hall. When they came out, papers had been signed and decisions were made. The decision which the two of them saw coming. It gave them a wave of relief rather than the sadness it should have. Dad was leaving and the two of them were in Ma's custody.

C H A P T E R   O N E:
Tyler and Ryan Godfrey
////------------------------------////

It was one of those nights in which Tyler couldn't sleep. His mind was plagued with thoughts of his brother and those pill bottles he had in his dresser. He was flipping through old pictures on his laptop of him and his brother. Family photos and school pictures and unexpected selfies.

He heard three soft knocks on his bedroom door. "Tyler? Are you awake?" The soft voice of his mother Charlotte Shepard shook him out of his thoughts.

Tyler muted his computer and rubbed his eyes sleepily. "Yeah, Mom, I'm up..." He stood up and wobbled over to his door, unlocking and opening it for her.

"Tyler, it's nearly midnight, why aren't you asleep?"

Tyler sighed. "I have a lot of things on my mind, Mom... Like Ryan..."

His mother lowered her head in understanding. She knew how hard Ryan's death was for everyone, but it especially took a toll on Tyler. They were twins, after all. They were connected in every way. Mrs. Shepard noticed the bags under her son's eyes. "What time have you been going to sleep?" Her son shrugged, putting his computer on his desk next to his pile of books.

Sighing, Mrs. Shepard pushed her son towards his bed. "Honey, I know you have a ton of school work that's piled up on you. Go to sleep and give your brain a rest."

Tyler just sat down on his bed while his mother ran around frantically trying to help her son. He couldn't go back to sleep, which was why he was up in the first place. He unplugged his phone from its charger and shuffled his favourite playlist. Plugging his headphones, he laid down on his bed listening to the song that started to play.

It was a song from Ryan's favourite band Imagine Dragons. For his and Tyler's fifteenth birthday, their parents bought them tickets to their concert, though it was nearly a month away. The two of them freaked out about being able to go.

Tyler smiled at the memory. His brother was always one for music and instruments. He was in the school band as the first chair saxophone player. He'd practice day and night to get ready for any upcoming concerts. Tyler would sit and listen to him play.

He heard a loud crash coming from the kitchen. He shot up out of bed, discarding his phone and music, and ran to the kitchen. When he arrived, his mother was sitting on the floor wearing her gardening gloves picking up the glass from the broken plate. "Mother," Tyler said, kneeling down next to her, "What happened?"

She rubbed her head sheepishly. "I was unloading the dishwasher and I dropped one of my good plates." She gestured to the glass shards lying on the floor. "At least, only one broke."

Tyler helped his mother pick up the glass and offered to help, but she insisted that he go back to bed. He protested saying he wasn't tired and could help, but she told him once he didn't have bags under his eyes she'd believe him. He turned back towards the direction of his bedroom hearing his music playing in the distance. When he entered the room, he realized it wasn't his room.

His eyes landed on the neatly made bed. No one had laid on it for three years now. The room smelled like apples and pencil shavings and had four unopened gifts laying on the desk. Tyler wanted to cry, but he made a promise. So, he bit his lip, wiped his eyes, and sat down on the white coloured rug that laid in the middle of the floor. He sighed and looked at the out-of-date calendar pinned to the wall. A date was circled in silver sharpie, February 28th. The birthday of the Godfrey twins. Tyler felt himself begin to tear up.

Ryan died just three days after their birthday. Those were the gifts Tyler gave him. Ryan never opened them. He had taken the gifts with a smile, thanking Tyler for them, but he never opened them. It was around that time he had started acting weird. Tyler never knew if it was his fault or not. Ryan stopped talking to him.

Tyler felt his tears fall onto his hands. He tried to repress his sobs, but they couldn't be held back anymore. His arms itched and he needed to get to that pill bottle. He heard loud footsteps pass by Ryan's old room. "Tyler! Are you in bed yet?"

He heard his mother open his bedroom door. She hummed in confusion and almost walked past again, but she caught Tyler sitting on the floor out of the corner of her eye. "Tyler? Honey?" she whispered, kneeling down next to him, "What's wrong?"

Tyler let out a strangled sob. "I miss Ryan, Mom... I miss him... So much..."

He felt his mother's arms wrap around him. "It's going to be okay, honey," she said, rubbing his back in a soothing manner. "Cheer up, Tyler... Ryan would want you to enjoy your birthday for him..."

Tyler's eyes widened. That's right.

Today was their birthday.

C H A P T E R   T W O:
Their Birthday
////-----------------------------////

When Tyler arrived at his high school that morning, he was immediately greeted by his childhood friend and girlfriend of four years, Melissa Edwards. She rushed over to Tyler and gently placed a beanie on his head. "Happy birthday, Ty!" she said, smiling happily.

Tyler sighed and forced a smile. "Thank you, Melissa." He gestured to the beanie that had been placed on his head. "What's this?"

Melissa clapped happily and grinned. "That's one of your many birthday presents from me. I had it custom-made!" She pointed to a symbol on the front of the hat. "That's the symbol of that band you like, right?"

Tyler took the beanie off and took a good look at the symbol. He ran his finger across the symbol. He nodded. "Yeah, it is. Thank you, I'll show this to Ryan when I visit him later today."

The hazel-haired female nodded and smiled sadly. "I guess you won't be doing anything for your birthday this year either, right?"

Tyler shook his head. "It just wouldn't be the same, Melissa. Sorry…" The loud ring of the school's bell interrupted the teens' conversation. Melissa pushed a strand of her hair behind her ear and waved her boyfriend off.

Tyler sat in his first-period class distracted and too conflicted by his emotions and memories to pay any attention to the class. He remembered when he and Ryan first started high school. They had both agreed to do half of their daily classes together and the other half by themselves. That same day they had both gotten into a fight with the seniors. Tyler and Ryan had won and while Bryan Shepard, their step-father, had congratulated them, Mother was quite angry at them for getting into a fight. Somehow the next day, they had received invitations to a senior party.

"Okay, class, I want you to do pages 426 and 430. Work on them until the bell rings; the rest is homework."

After hearing the class groan, Tyler chuckled at imagining Ryan finishing both pages before the bell rang. Tyler didn't bother to start working on the assignment; he'd get it done after he visited Ryan. He rested his head on the desk, welcoming the coldness of the metal to soothe his headache. His eyelids started to droop shut. He didn't have the strength to stay awake anymore. After being awake all night, reminiscing on the memories of the past, all he wanted at that moment was to sleep without any distractions.

~~~ February 28th, 2014~~~

"-Happy birthday dear Tyler and Ryan! Happy birthday to you~!"

The many family members cheered and clapped in excitement as the two boys blew out the candles on their silver and gold cake. Ryan turned to Tyler with a wide grin on his face. "What'd you wish for, Ty?"

"That your wish came true. What'd you wish for, Ry?"

The younger one chuckled. "That your wish came true."

Their mother placed plates of cake in front of them. "There you go, boys. Enjoy!" The two nodded and said their thanks. "Man, we're cheesy brothers, aren't we?" Tyler said, scooping up some cake. Ryan nodded and smiled sweetly, doing the same as Tyler. "But you love it."

Tyler laughed, nearly choking on his cake. "Yes, it is an intriguing quality."

The two looked around at their family members laughing and chatting with one another happily. Ryan felt a light poke on his shoulder. "Yeah, Tyler?" He asked, turning towards his brother. Tyler smiled. "Happy birthday, Ry."

Ryan smiled back at him, a sad glint in his eyes. "Yeah… Happy birthday, Ty."

It was a look Tyler never forgot.

It was the same look on the face of his dying body.

And then it just froze like that.

~~~~~~~

Tyler shot up out of his chair in fear. The students and teacher stared at him with confused or annoyed expressions. "Mr. Godfrey, is everything alright?" The teacher, Mr. Grant, looked at him with worry showing on his face. Tyler began to stumble backward, tripping on some stray textbooks and falling to the floor. A few students of the class stood up from their chairs to try and see what was happening. "Mr. Godfrey!" Mr. Grant rushed over to the fallen boy and kneeled down to render aid. Tyler's breathing was rushed, he had broken into a cold sweat; the teacher had no idea what was happening.

His arms itched - *he itched*. He wanted to scratch them - *where did he put those pills*.

Tyler's arms were crossed and his fingernails were digging into his elbows, nearly breaking the skin. Tyler could hear the teacher and a few students calling out to him faintly, but his body wouldn't acknowledge them. He slowly moved one hand to cover his mouth. He could feel the bile in his body threatening to spill out of him. They were still calling out to him, asking, 'is he okay?' or 'what's happening?' and 'should I call 911'. Tyler gripped his stomach and bent over his knees. He couldn't hold anything in any longer.

He ignored the hand on his shoulder, his teacher telling him to attempt to get to the garbage can; before he knew it, he was throwing up.

Tyler blacked out after that. He awoke in the infirmary of the school. He had an ice pack on his forehead and bandages on his elbows. He attempted to sit up, but a gentle voice coming from the left of him told him to stay still. Tyler turned towards the voice in confusion. There sat a boy around his age with shaggy blonde hair and a blue t-shirt. "You should stay still," he said, "The nurse said if you move too much you might get sick again."

Nodding, Tyler put the ice pack on the table next to the infirmary bed and laid back down. "Your name's Tyler, right?" the blonde asked.

Tyler weakly nodded and groaned from the movement.

"I'm Felix," he said standing up from his seat, "I-I'm a junior, too. I was heading into second-period science and a few teachers were gathered around you, trying to wake you up. I offered to bring you to the infirmary. They thought I wouldn't be able to carry you, but you're actually quite light. Very light actually… Um…" Felix noticed how he began to rant and slowly trailed off.

He looked over his shoulder out the window at the multitude of high schoolers outside for gym. An awkward silence was left in the air, then Felix realized Tyler was asleep again. The blonde shook Tyler awake, apologizing for irritating him. "You shouldn't fall asleep again, Tyler," he said, "Your mother will be coming to get you soon. Mr. Grant called her a little while ago."

Tyler sat up slowly and nodded to signal that he acknowledged his words. "How long was I out?" he asked.

Felix sat on the edge of the infirmary bed and counted invisible numbers with his eyes. "Not long… Your mother said she was at a meeting and your father had to go to a nearby city for an interview."

"Ah, okay…" Tyler ran his fingers through his hair and sighed loudly. He didn't bother correcting Felix's noun to 'Step-father'. He began to get out of the bed, but Felix stopped him.

"You shouldn't move around too much; as said before, we don't know if you might throw up again," Felix warned.

Tyler smiled. "I'll be fine." Tyler figured he could be embarrassed about puking in first period later. He didn't have the craving for those pills anymore.

Felix put his hands in his pockets and stood up from the bed. Tyler stood up and stretched his arms high until you could hear them crack. He turned to the blonde who stood a few feet away from him. "Thanks for bringing me here. I don't even know how you were able to pick me up-"

"About that…" Felix said, scratching his neck, "You're really skinny, y'know. I'm guessing you don't eat much…"

"Yeah… I don't eat a whole lot. I-I guess I just don't… have the appetite." Tyler looked at the blonde with sadness clouding his eyes. His mind conflicted by the memories of his past.

Felix stood in front of him, an understanding smile playing on his features. "Why don't you have an appetite? My mom says that a certain event in one's life can cause unhealthy eating habits. Do you have any girlfriend troubles or misguided family members or maybe you've experienced the death of a loved one?" Tyler had heard this line of questioning before in those counseling sessions his mother forced him to go to.

Tyler nodded slowly, not sure if he should trust Felix. "The last one. My, uh, my brother. A couple of years back."

"So that's what this is about, your brother?" Felix asked. "Why is this time sensitive for you if he died a few years back?"

"Well, uh… We were twins, so it's a bit different." Tyler said, tears spiking his eyes. "My brother died just a few days after our fifteenth birthday…" He wiped his eyes and chuckled a bit. "He'd be seventeen with me today. So it's kind of a big deal for me and my family…"

"I'm sorry… You must miss him, huh?"

"Yeah." Tyler nodded. "A day doesn't go by without me thinking about him… He was my best friend just as much as he was my brother."

Suddenly the door of the infirmary burst open and Tyler's mother ran through the room and immediately went to her son. She cupped his face and forcefully tilted his head from side to side. "Are you alright?! Are you hurt?!" she asked, panting slightly from running part of the way there.

Tyler gave her a small smile. "I'm alright, Mom. A little woozy, sure, but other than that I'm okay."

His mother sighed in relief before turning to Felix. "Who is this?" she asked.

He looked confused for a moment, before realizing his mother was talking about Felix. "Oh, that's Felix. He's the one who brought me here after I passed out."

Mrs. Shepard's mouth formed an 'o' shape. "Ah, well, thank you for watching over my son, Felix…?"

"Oh, Strand. Felix Strand. It's nice to meet you, Mrs. Godfrey."

Mrs. Godfrey turned back to her son and tapped on his shoulder. "We should invite him to dinner," she whispered to him, "Y'know as a 'thank you'."

Tyler nodded in agreement and walked over to Felix. "Hey, can I get your phone number? My mother and I would like to treat you for helping me."

The blonde smiled nervously. "You don't have to-"

"No," Mrs. Shepard interrupted him, "We insist."

Felix sighed in defeat. "Okay then."

The two boys exchanged numbers and then went their own separate ways. Felix to his current class and Tyler went with his mother back home. The car ride back to the familiar childhood home was quick and quiet. The two The two of them didn't say anything to one another and Tyler didn't have the strength to turn up the faintly playing music that was coming from the radio. It was only when Mrs. Shepard pulled into their driveway anyone spoke. "Tyler, are you sure you're okay?" She asked, "Are you tired at all? Do feel like you're going to throw up anymore? How about-"

"Mom."

Tyler looked his mother dead in the eyes with a small, sad smile. "I miss him, Mom. It's supposed to be our birthday, and everyone I talk to at school keeps using the word 'your'. It's not mine, Mom. It's ours." Tears started to form in his eyes. "I just want to see him alive and happy, even if it's just one last time."

His mother hugged him tightly, wiping the tears flowing down his face with her thumb. "Would you like to go visit him? I'll let you borrow the car… Your father and I will visit him later, okay?"

Tyler hugged her back and nodded at her offer. That's all he wanted at that moment. He wanted to see his brother. He wanted it to be their birthday again. Not his. He wanted it to be Ryan and Tyler's birthday. He wanted everything to go back to normal. He wanted his brother by his side again.

He felt his mother running her fingers through his hair in a comforting manner. "Don't think too much, Ty. Just go see him." She pulled away and started the car once again. "I'm going to go inside, okay?"

Tyler nodded and gave her a small smile. "Okay."

C H A P T E R   T H R E E:
Recollection
////-----------------------------////

He was glad his mother let him use the car. A little while back, Tyler had hidden one of those pill bottles in a compartment behind his mother's makeup and sunglasses. He took a couple of pills before driving off, almost instantly relaxing due to the pill's chemical composition. His mother didn't want him going on the medicine, but Tyler knew he needed it. The citalopram didn't work often, but it just made him nauseous and gave him insomnia, which is why he didn't take it every day as instructed. Tyler took Xanax most of the time to help calm him. It didn't last too long, though, so he had to take it many times during the day

When Tyler arrived at the cemetery, he just calmly stood by his parent's car. On the drive here, he received multiple texts from Melissa about the party she had planned for him. He turned his phone off and tightly gripped the three white roses in his hand. White roses were Ryan's favourite. He said the colour white was his favourite; it represented purity and cleanliness, two things Ryan believed lacked in this generation. Roses were considered a symbol of balance, something the twins had valued greatly. The white rose itself represented true love in early tradition, but that title has been taken over by the red rose.

Tyler smiled at the memory and continued to walk through the gates of the cemetery known to the town as Toxteth Park Cemetery. He walked for a few minutes before arriving at Ryan's grave.

Ryan Rhett Godfrey
2000~2015
Son, brother & friend

Before the gravestone was a cobblestone vase filled with three dying white roses. Tyler lifted the dying roses and replaced them with the new ones. Three was Ryan's favourite number. Three refers to the Trinity. The number means you are receiving protection, help, and guidance. Tyler wanted to honour everything Ryan favoured, though he couldn't include everything.

Tyler felt the dying roses start to crumble under his fingers. He sat down in front of his brother's gravestone and sadly smiled. "Hey, Ryan…" he said, "Happy Birthday. We're seventeen now."

He stared at the gravestone, awaiting an answer that would never come. "Do you remember the gift Ma got us for our fifteenth birthday? That book of constellations, remember? And, those decoder rings were pretty cool, huh? From, uh, Aunt Cass? I still have yours… Along with all the other gifts we got that year. Like the drumstick pencils Dad sent us… You used those for your drumset at home and you'd bring them to school to use during our study hall. You were always Mrs. Erin's favourite student."

Silence filled the air. Tyler continued, "You were a great percussionist, but no matter how much you played the drums you still loved the saxophone more. I could never get any better at the drums; I guess that's why everyone told me to stick to strings, huh?"

Silence.

"I don't know about you, but I still can't believe we actually got a prize at the seventh-grade talent show. I swear, we sucked, but they said we did good... And I guess we didn't need to practice so much, but y'know what they say, twins have a special bond."

Tyler knew he'd never get an answer from his brother again, but he knew what Ryan would say. 'We never were able to use the decoder rings' or 'We were pretty great with the drums and guitar'. They were a team. They did everything together. Tyler liked to think about what life would be like if he were still alive. What it would be like if Tyler got to the rooftop in time.

Tyler let his fingers ghost over his brother's name on the gravestone. He wrote Ryan's name with his fingers in as many ways as he could think of. He was stalling; he didn't want to leave. He didn't want to wander back into the real world. He didn't want to deal with Melissa when he told her he didn't plan on celebrating his birthday anymore. He didn't want to go to the party she planned. He didn't want to leave his brother.

He knew if Ryan was still there he'd tell Tyler to make some friends, to let loose, to have some fun. Tyler didn't think he was able to have as much fun anymore because his mind would wander to his brother and how much fun it would be if they had done it together.

"Mother and Bryan will come to visit you soon, okay?" He whispered.

Instead of waiting for the nonexistent answer to come, he stood up after turning his phone on and took a picture of himself and his brother's gravestone. He knew the picture would seem weird to other people, but to him, it was signifying their previous birthdays together. It was their tradition; no matter the circumstances they'd take a picture together every year on their birthday.

Ignoring the ringing coming from his phone, he turned to the gravestone once more and whispered a small goodbye. "I love you, Ryan," he said with a smile forming on his face, "Happy seventeenth birthday."

He stood by the car for a bit with a pill bottle in hand. Tyler opened it and poured two pills into his hand. With a large swig of water, he swallowed them both. After waiting for the pills to kick in, he got into the car.

The teen started his parents' car and drove to the party Melissa had planned for him, despite how much the medicine was affecting him.

The party was being held at the Liverpool Aquatics Centre. Tyler sighed. She knew he didn't like to swim. The drive to the aquatics centre took a little less than five minutes with light traffic even when taking the fastest route.

When he arrived, he saw multiple unfamiliar cars parked outside. He walked inside looking left and right, trying to figure out where everyone was. He was about to call Melissa, but a familiar face walked around the corner.

"Tyler!" he said, "Welcome!"

The teen's clothes were soaked and his eyes were red, most likely from the chlorine. "Hey Felix," Tyler said, "Where's everybody?"

"That way," He said gesturing towards the room he came from.

No sound was coming from the room, which confused Tyler, but he decided to ignore it. "Why are your clothes all wet?" he asked the blonde.

"Oh," He smiled awkwardly, "My friends pushed me in the pool. I came out here so I could look for some towels since we're out of them in there."

Tyler nodded in understanding. "Y'know where towels are?"

Felix chuckled and shook his head. "Nope, but since you're here, you can help me look for them."

The two teens wandered the hallways searching the rooms for towels they could bring back to the pool for the other people Melissa invited to use. They had managed to find a few before finally giving up. As they walked back to the main room for the party, Tyler asked the blonde a few questions. "Hey, who else is here? When I got here there was a bunch of other cars I had never seen before."

"Um… I believe Melissa invited whoever she had in her contacts list. I had overheard a group of girls talking about it earlier."

"I guess this really was a last-minute party…" Tyler mumbled to himself.

"Last-minute?" Felix repeated, turning towards Tyler with a confused look. "Melissa has been planning this pool party for nearly three weeks. When everyone got here, she said there was a change of plans, though I wasn't able to hear what those were exactly."

"Ah," Tyler chuckled, "So the birthday part of it was last-minute."

Felix laughed along with him. "I guess so."

The two turned the corner into the locker room where a multitude of bags was with clothes and makeup or phones overflowing out of them. As they walked deeper into the locker room they heard echoes of laughter and shouting closer and clearer. When they entered the pool room the harsh scent of chlorine hit their senses.

"Tyler!!" A loud female voice emitted from the far end of the pool. Melissa carefully jogged over to Tyler and Felix, smiling sweetly. "Happy Birthday!!" she shouted with a grin plastered on her face.

Tyler forced a smile. "T-thanks, Melissa…"

Felix noticed and quickly tried to end the conversation before it started. "Melissa, where should we put these towels? There's not many, but it's all we could find."

She turned to him with a slightly annoyed expression, but quickly put on a smile. "You can put them on the towel racks by the table with the cake and stuff." She pointed to the table with her hand clearly shaking.

"Thank you, Melissa." Felix nudged Tyler with his elbow and they continued to bring the towels to their appropriate destination. The two set them on the towel racks and sat down in nearby chairs. Tyler chuckled to himself. "Something funny?" The blonde asked, running his fingers through his still wet hair.

Tyler shook his head. "Ryan did that same thing."

"Excuse me?" Felix asked, not following.

"Ryan could tell when I was annoyed or uncomfortable and he'd get me out of it if he could…"

"Ah…" Felix now realized that he was referring to their previous conversation with Melissa. "You don't seem to like her, y'know."

"I do, it's just…" He thought for a moment, struggling to find the words to describe the situation. "She keeps on trying to get me to do things for my birthday. 'Get over it' she says… Well, it's easier said than done."

"Sounds annoying."

Tyler stifled a laugh. "It is."

The two sat in a comfortable silence while listening to the incoherent shouts and splashes of the pool. Tyler felt his eyelids begin to droop shut. He forced them open and stood up from the chair.

"What's up?" Felix asked, watching him get up.

Tyler ran his fingers through his hair and sighed. "I'm getting tired…"

The blonde gave Tyler a small smile. "How can you even remotely be tired with all this noise?"

"No idea," Tyler sat back down and began to fidget with his fingers. "Ryan used to tell me how weird it was that I could fall asleep nearly anywhere."

"Hm…" Felix relaxed in his chair, leaning back fully, looking at Tyler with an intrigued expression.

"What?" Tyler tilted his head in confusion.

"You are comparing me to your brother a lot…" He said.

Tyler scratched the back of his neck. "Have I? I-I'm sorry…"

Felix waved his hands around apologetically. "No, it's not that. Um…" He struggled to find the right words. "I guess, I act like him…?"

Tyler looked at the ground with a sad glint in his eyes. He laced his hands together and sighed. Felix and Ryan acted quite alike now that he thought about it. Was he replacing Ryan with Felix? He gulped nervously. "N-no… Not at all…"

The blonde stared at Tyler, who was now resting his head in his hands and ruffling his hair in an irritated and frustrated manner. "Ty? Are you alright?"

Tyler put his hand over his mouth and made a muffled gagging noise. Was the medicine wearing off? "Tyler!? Are you okay? Talk to me, man." Felix kneeled in front of him and put his hands on his shoulders and rubbed them in a comforting manner. "Tylor?!"

Ryan used to call him Ty. He gave him that nickname.

Don't call me that.

He felt the non-existent digested food crawl up his throat.

Please don't make this worse.

He was going to throw up again. He could hear Felix faintly calling his name. He could see blurry figures crowd around him. Tyler looked around the room frantically searching for a garbage can or something he could vomit in, but as he looked around...

Tyler could swear he saw Ryan standing on the other side of the pool.

C H A P T E R   F O U R:
Dead or Alive
////------------------------------////

Ryan remembered dying, even if just for a moment. He remembered the feeling of thirst and hunger dissipate from his body, not being able to speak and losing his vision. He felt the pain of hitting the ground at a high velocity for a few seconds before his body went numb. He couldn't hear anything anymore and he couldn't taste any of the food he had eaten earlier. Ryan had a brief moment to think about Tyler and what would happen to him, but then he felt relaxed and his mind went blank.

He died.

He was fully aware of that...

So, why did he wake up?

When he had awoken, he heard multiple men talking nearby. His hearing wasn't that great, but he could make out a few words here and there.

".... If unsuccessful... undead... exterminate... failure again..."

He had begun to regain his senses After a while, he began to feel the cold of the metal below him. Ryan mustered the strength he had regained and sat up on the metal table. His head was spinning and his vision was blurry. He was in a hospital gown. *Am I in a hospital...?* He looked around the room and tried to make out the furniture. He saw greyish, rectangular blobs with a bright light emitting from the middle of it. *A… monitor?*

Ryan attempted to stand up and failed. His legs were weak and his chest felt sore. "H… He…" He couldn't speak, his throat too was dry. Ryan started to bang on the metal table as loud as he could. He heard faint footsteps coming from his left; they kept getting louder and louder until they stopped. Ryan saw large feet next to him.

He kneeled next to Ryan and tapped his shoulder. "Hey there," the muffled male voice said, "Where'd you come from?"

Ryan tried to say something, but all that came out was small croaks and hums

The man chuckled. "Can't speak… Do you know sign language?"

Ryan shook his head.

"Morse code?"

Ryan tried to recall if he had ever learned morse code. Once, he had recalled he and Tyler learned it while camping, he nodded slowly. The man sighed. "I'm guessing you have some questions…?"

He lifted his shaky hand and began to tap in morse code for the one major question he had on his mind. Ryan watched the man's expressions changed as he tried to decipher the code he had laid out. Once he had figured it out, his eyes grew large and grinned widely.

'Why am I alive?'

..

..

..

..

..

..

To the rest of the world, he was known as Zander White's adopted son, Séan Stefansson, but to the scientists of Nico Global, he was known as their one success. Ryan walked the earth as a resurrected teen. He was supposed to be dead, he knew that much. The reason for his being alive was still not very clear. He knew the gist of it; Zander, with seven other team members, were experimenting on the possibility of resurrection. Ryan was their only success out of fifteen corpses.

In order to figure out what they did differently to Ryan, they kept him here. Nearly three years and they still hadn't figured it out. All Ryan wanted was to go home, but he couldn't. They couldn't know he was alive. As Zander puts it, they can't know until they can perfect it.

Ryan has been posing as his adopted son for nearly three years. Posing as Séan Stefansson. He hates it. Ryan hates it. He just wants to go home. He wants to see his family. His brother. He wants to help his brother get off the medication he keeps overdosing on. He wants to be Ryan Godfrey again.

"Séan? When did you decide to come back from boarding school in California?"

That's right. Zander brought him and his daughter to some big interview on the White family. Ryan put on a fake smile. "Well, I had heard that my big sister had finals coming up, I just had to be here to support her. And while I'm here I want to finish high school locally."

The reporters nodded and wrote down what he said in their notebooks. They turned to his adoptive sister. "Nicole, how did you feel when you heard your brother was coming home?"

The teen clapped her hands happily. "I was ecstatic! I hadn't seen Séan in nearly a year, so when Dad told me he was coming home, I cooked his favourite meals and planned a bunch of things for us to do. We had so much fun!!"

Ryan glanced at Nicole and sighed. "I did indeed have fun, Nicole."

Photographers were taking pictures, interviewers were writing things down and asking questions left and right. Ryan was tired of this. He wanted to sleep. He wanted to lay down and listen to some music. He hated the flashing of the cameras, the indistinct voices, and the fake cheerful voices and smiles.

When it was done, Zander took his 'children' home. Zander went to his office; he still had another conference with the other scientists who experimented on Ryan. They often had conferences. Sometimes, they asked Ryan to participate, as well, but most of the time he wasn't included.

"Ryan?" Nicole was standing in front of him with her hands on her hips and her reading glasses on. "Did Dad give you your class schedule?" Zander had enrolled Ryan in the same high school Tyler was in. Zander asked to put Ryan in classes that Tyler wasn't in. If they were in the same class, Ryan would want to talk to him and that would present too many problems.

Ryan nodded. "Yeah, he said he put it on my desk. I'll check over it tonight."

Nicole adjusted her glasses and left for her bedroom. She was in college now, so the only times Ryan ever saw her was when Zander scheduled interviews or something. He watched her as she entered her bedroom and sighed angrily. This was tiring.

The teen heard a faint ding coming from his room. He walked inside and opened up his computer. On the top left corner of the screen was a small rectangular box that read Liverpool Aquatics Centre. Clicking on it, Ryan listened to the audio that emitted from the computer's speakers.

"Ryan did that same thing."

That was Tyler's voice. Who was he talking to?

"Excuse me?"

Who was that?

"Ryan could tell when I was annoyed or uncomfortable and he'd get me out of it if he could…"

Ryan smiled at the memory. They may have been twins, but people always found Tyler the slightest bit more attractive than Ryan. Girls were always trying to flirt with him. When Tyler and Melissa started dating, she was always trying to get Tyler to ditch Ryan. He never did cave though; he was true to his word.

"Ah… You don't seem to like her y'know."

"I do, it's just… She keeps on trying to get me to do things for my birthday. 'Get over it' she says… Well, it's easier said than done."

Melissa was always so pushy. Even when they were kids. She always bossed the two boys around, trying to get them to do what she wanted. It's annoying, even now.

"Sounds annoying."

There's that other voice again. Who was that?

Ryan heard Tyler laugh. **"It is."**

The brunette said nothing and listened to the muffled shouts and laughs in the background. Neither voices spoke for about three minutes before Ryan heard Tyler sigh heavily.

That other voice spoke first. **"What's up?"**

Tyler sighed again. **"I'm getting tired..."**

Ryan chuckled. He always got tired in the weirdest places. Once at a concert, then at Comic-Con, then in a multitude of other places. When he used to ask Tyler why he got tired in the places with a whole lot of noise, he'd always say the same thing, 'I find it calming'.

"How can you even be remotely tired with all this noise?"

"No idea... Ryan used to tell me how weird it was that I could fall asleep nearly anywhere."

A shiver went down Ryan's back. He muted the conversation between Tyler and that mystery voice and went to find his sneakers. He put them on quickly, not bothering to tie the laces. He grabbed a sweatshirt and ran out the door of the White residence.

Something was wrong.

He could feel it pooling in the pit of his stomach; he knew something was up. Tyler must've been using again. Ryan knew how he could get when he was coming down from a high. It was an emotional roller coaster for both of them despite the fact Ryan and Tyler were nowhere near one another.

He ran as fast as he could to the Aquatics Centre. It wasn't too far from Zander's house, but he wanted to get there as quickly as possible. When he arrived, he dashed through the hallway, looking for the room with the most people. He heard multiple voices coming from a room around the corner. Running into the room, he pushed past the people sitting in the locker room and slid to a stop when he reached the pool.

Tyler was on the floor on the other side of the pool.

Ryan knew something was wrong.

He had to force himself not to run over there. He couldn't be seen by Tyler. Ryan put his hands in the pockets of his sweatshirt and watched the scene from the opposite side of the pool. People were trying to help him up, help calm him down. They were asking what's wrong.

Ryan wanted to stay and see if he would be alright, but Tyler looked up at him.

He could see his green eyes widen at the sight of him. It caused him to pass out. Before Ryan left, he took a picture of the people over there. One that caught his eye was a blonde. He had his hand on Tyler's shoulder and looked genuinely concerned for his brother. Something told Ryan that was the voice.

He'd ask Zander to identify him later.

For now, he needed to leave.

C H A P T E R   F I V E:
Mirror
////-----------------------------////

Ryan decided not to go back to Zander's house. If he asked him to identify the blonde, Zander would know he left without permission. He could explain everything later, but right now he needed answers. Ryan had a friend he made whilst being locked up in the lab for a few months after awakening. An informant who was helping his father investigate Nico Global whilst passing information onto the company. He went by the name Royce. They had only talked on the phone using a voice modulator or through email, but he had been a great help. The one friend he managed to make wore a mask. One that he refused to let anyone see through.

"Royce," He whispered, after arriving in an alleyway near the high school, "I need help."

"With what?" Royce said, static covering his voice.

"I need a name."

"There's so many names out there, Godfrey."

"Um… Facial recognition. I need you to run a picture through facial recognition."

For a moment or two, the male on the other end of the line was silent. "Send me the picture; I'll give you what I can find, alright?"

"Alright. Thank you, Royce."

Ryan listened to the static that filled the other end of the line. Royce said nothing as he ended the call and left Ryan alone in the silence of the alleyway. He sent Royce the picture of the person he saw with Tyler earlier today. He knew he wouldn't get any information until late tomorrow, but he wanted it as soon as possible.

He heard a car screech to a stop next to him. Glancing to the side, he identified it as belonging to Zander. The window rolled down to reveal the man's shadowed face and his unruly grey hair. "Ryan," he said, "I thought I asked you not to leave without telling me."

The teen glared at Zander, showing his annoyance. "I wanted some time without those 'babysitters' of yours." Ryan was referring to the bodyguards Zander assigned to keep an eye on him. He found it annoying.

"Cameron and Will are nice guys, why do you hate them so much?"

For a moment, Ryan said nothing. "It's not them I hate."

The scientist sighed. "I know, I know. Listen, Ryan, we're close to figuring it out… We just need a little bit more time."

"Define a little," he huffed in annoyance.

"Maybe less than three months… After that, we'll send you home and explain everything to your family, and you can continue to live a normal life with your addict of a brother."

Ryan huffed at Zander's insult to Tyler. He opened the door to the car and sat in the seat across from Zander. They started to drive towards the White's residence, which should have been fairly quick, but traffic was busy that night. Ryan looked out the window and stared at the numerous lights of the cars around them. The sounds of rumbling engines and car horns seemed so calming. The rustling of papers snapped the teen out of his trance. Ryan turned towards Zander and watched as he looked over numerous files that most likely consisted of medical records and personal information of unknown people.

Ryan sighed loudly. Noticing this, Zander set his papers down and folded his hands in an interested manner. "What's up?"

The teen's eyes narrowed. "Knowing you, I probably don't have any classes with Tyler. I'd like to know why."

Zander knew Ryan well enough to know he wasn't making a request. It was a command. "Your family can't know it's you when you arrive; I'll be taking any necessary precautions to make sure they don't realize it's you. He's your twin, so if you two see one another it's very likely he'll recognize you."

He grit his teeth in anger. "So I can't even see my brother when I'm wearing that stupid disguise of yours?!"

Zander's eyes widened at the sudden outburst from the usually very calm teen. "Ryan," Zander said calmly, "We're close." He tapped the pile of papers next to him. "We're so close to figuring out what we did to make your heart beat again." A smile began to appear on his face. "We just need a little more time."

Ryan let the childish ignorance of his mind to get the better of him. "Please, figure it out as quickly as you can. I want to leave as soon as possible."

Nodding, Zander began to look through his files once more. He had an oddly calm smile on his face; the cold look in his eyes didn't match his smile at all. It seemed menacing, somehow. Ryan paid no mind to it and continued to stare out the window of the slow-moving car once more. The quiet atmosphere in the car lulled the teen into a dream-like state of mind. He smiled internally as he remembered how much Tyler hated the quiet. It seemed uncomfortable to him, while to Ryan it was the heaven he fears he'll never reach.

There's a part of him that believes he'll never see his family again.

He's tried to ignore it, but it bubbles back up when Zander begins speaking about 'figuring it out'. When Zander says that, he'll have a small breakthrough and immediately plummet downward in terms of progress.

Hope is just something he finds so little of these days.

His mind wandered over the memories of his childhood, eventually landing during the time his parents got divorced. His father was a kind man, but he failed to keep his honest thoughts to himself. He lost jobs easily, and Mother had gotten fed up and decided to divorce him. Ryan and Tyler thought they were going to be separated; thankfully, the court allowed them to stay with their mother. They haven't seen their father since then.

Apparently, Mother had remarried some man named Bryan. Ryan was worried about the kind of person he could be, but after doing a background check through Royce, he determined Bryan was a kind man. Mother had chosen well. Ryan felt no need to conduct a face-to-face investigation.

Ryan smiled, still looking out the window. Royce had sent him his mother's most recent wedding picture; Tyler, Mother, and Bryan were wearing goofy smiles with cake frosting covering their cheeks and fingers.

Ryan felt the car pull to a stop. He crooked his head toward Zander, who had put all of his papers back into his bag, and sighed in a frustrated way. "The car stopped, Zander. Let's go already."

He could hear the man chuckle as he began to gather his things. "Yeah, yeah…" He got out of the car and grabbed his bag. "We've got a few more tests to run before you can go to bed, though, so don't get too relaxed."

Ryan got out of the car, grabbed his phone, and checked for any texts. "I'm never relaxed… Especially here."

Zander knew that very well, but he chose to ignore it.

The next day Ryan woke up with sore arms covered in bloodied bandages. Those tests ran too long, and he didn't get enough sleep, which wasn't helpful since he was supposed to start school today. He wore a long sweater to cover up the bandages, but they were still slightly visible. Zander had even taken blood from his forehead; he combed his hair in a certain way so it would cover the mark the needle had left. The fake glasses he was given also helped.

His disguise wasn't something big and extravagant. He grew his hair out over the years and styled differently than his brother. A beauty mark under his mouth and contacts to make his irises a different colour.

Ryan looked in the mirror, slightly disoriented since he hadn't been 'Séan' in a while. He knew it was necessary, the disguise. He decided to be stubborn, of course, he didn't know why that was the immediate attitude his mind went to, but it certainly was helpful at sometimes.

"Ryan!! We've got to go!!" He heard Nicole shout from the kitchen.

"Alright!!" He shouted back, slightly annoyed.

He hurried to school. The same high school he went to three years ago. The place where 'Ryan' died. He would now come back but as 'Séan'. A part of him hoped Tyler wouldn't notice him, but the other wanted to see him as soon as possible. He wanted to tell him he was alive; he wanted him to know all of the things he had endured throughout the years. He was going to be 'Ryan' again soon. He had a strong feeling telling him so. He'll be with his family soon. He'll be with Tyler.

When he arrived at the school, paparazzi were surrounding the car Zander prepared for Ryan. Cameras were flashing, people were chattering; the talking wouldn't stop. It would all be over soon. He just had to get through the day. He walked into the building, ignoring everyone who asked questions.

The building was full of students, and thankfully, they didn't pester him with questions. He was looking for the blonde he saw with Tyler the other day. He'd ask him to be his guide for the day so he could do an 'evaluation' of him himself. Well, until Royce sent him the documents of him.

Ryan looked around the building. His eyes traced the rows of lockers lining the walls, carefully and quickly studying each student he passed by. None of them matched the picture. He couldn't find him. Ryan pulled out his cell phone to see if there was any news from Royce.

Nothing from him and that other guy was nowhere to be found.

Running his fingers through his hair in frustration, Ryan walked through multiple hallways in search of this blonde he saw with his brother. Just then, the bad feeling he had felt the other day was slowly growing stronger and more apparent.

He turned the corner and went into the restroom. He looked in the mirror on the far side of the room. His hair was all over the place from when he messed with it earlier. The glasses were foggy and crooked. He felt as if he were going crazy.

The bathroom door opened and it echoed throughout the almost empty room. Ryan ignored the sound of footsteps getting closer as he turned to leave. But he was met with a sight he didn't expect to see.

He gasped quietly and began to study the person in front of him. He had to force himself not to run up to him and hug him and tell him how much he missed him.

But he couldn't do anything at that moment. He could only stand there in awe and whisper…

"…Tyler."

C H A P T E R   S I X:

Reunion
////----------------------------////

"...Tyler."

Ryan stood in front of his brother, awe clearly written all over him. For a few moments, they both just stood there, staring at one another. Confusion painted Tyler's face. He had an eyebrow raised and his nose was scrunched up as if he had smelled something unpleasant.

"Did you say something?" The older of the two asked.

Ryan said nothing but stared at his brother. He couldn't speak. The words he had been wanting to say had completely disappeared from his mind. It was either that or a part of him knew he couldn't risk it. Who knows what Zander could do to his family if he found out they'd been interacting?

The younger one looked up at Tyler, his eyes starting to tear up. Concern began to form on Tyler's face. "Is something wrong?" he asked, his voice wavering just the tiniest bit.

Ryan pushed past his brother and out the door. He ran through the long hallways of the high school, sliding between students and teachers. He knew his brother wasn't chasing him - Ryan was just afraid he would chase after Tyler.

The teen looked around, now realizing he was outside. He was by the soccer field bleachers. He sat down, running his hands through his hair and sighing loudly. He couldn't do it. There was no way he could wait to see his family now. Not with Tyler everywhere he went.

Ryan took in the scenery of the sports fields, watching the students do their assigned exercises and whatnot. He was never one for sports, but he did find them enjoyable to watch. It was orchestrated beautifully imperfect.

A small ding emitted from Ryan's phone. It was a message from Royce with a file attached.

His name's Felix Kyle Strand. Don't mess this up, Godfrey. You can't afford it.

Ryan stood up from the bleachers. Now he had something to take his mind off of Tyler. It was the one he considered his replacement.

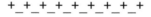

Tyler stared at the door as it slowly shut, the loud thunk of it echoing through the empty restroom. Something was off about that student. He didn't know what it was, but he seemed… familiar. Tyler had never seen the teen before, but something about him lit a fire deep in his chest. Igniting the light that was the ashes of his once happy family.

He looked kinda like Ryan. Tyler knew that was impossible - Ryan was dead. He couldn't change that. But that student seemed so much like him.

Tyler shook his head. He was hallucinating, and he knew it. Yesterday he supposedly saw his dead brother, and now it seems everyone portrays the same physical attributes of him. As disturbing as it was, he knew he had to keep telling himself that Ryan was dead.

He grasped what death meant.

Death meant you as a person disappeared

Most people think it's your problems that disappear, while in all reality you cease to exist.

It seems everyone forgot about Ryan. His picture was still hanging on the wall of the hallway. Actually, there's a few of them here and there. Tyler liked that the teachers wanted to honour him by putting up his picture, but nowadays most people at this school have zero ideas who he is. People move away, new people move in their place. They're replaced. They're all replaced.

Like how Tyler's replacing Ryan with Felix.

He shook his head, taking a couple of pills from the bottle in his jacket pocket. Tyler sighed loudly and exited the restroom. There was a small crowd around the water fountains and the rows of lockers nearby, but they didn't make too much noise. He began to walk to his first-period class, glancing at all the people around him. Suddenly, he felt a light tap on his shoulder. "'Sup, Tyler!"

Tyler looked at the blonde who stood before him. "Hey, Felix."

The two started to talk as they made their way to their respective classrooms. There was a point when Tyler stopped listening to what Felix was saying and began to think about everything that's been going on. One thing he knew and dreaded.

He was trying to replace Ryan. It wasn't his intention to do so. He just wanted a friend. Ryan would want him to have a friend -

Tyler stopped walking, allowing Felix to walk farther in front of him. He stopped when he noticed Tyler wasn't walking anymore, forcing other students to walk around him. "Tyler, are you alright?"

He didn't say anything. He just stared at Felix. Tyler didn't want to be friends with Felix if it meant giving Ryan up. "No…" He whispered, slowly shaking his head.

Tyler didn't want to forget about his little brother.

"I'm not okay, Felix."

He was the worst.

"Nothing's alright…"

He kept shaking his head.

"I'm...."

...Disgusting.

"Leave me alone…"

Felix stood there, shocked. "What..?" Despite Tyler's request, Felix still attempted to calm him down.

Tyler's eyes began to well up with tears. "Leave me alone… please..." Did he not take enough pills earlier? For a moment, Tyler debated grabbing the pill bottle from his pocket.

He decided against it, thinking he was going to vomit. Tyler's hands began to crawl up over his mouth preemptively covering the bile's escape. His tears became heavier, thus falling down his cheeks. "Get away from me…" He said, his voice muffled.

Felix had concern written on his face. He slowly walked up to Tyler, not fully grasping the situation but having the slightest idea. "Tyler…" The blonde put a hand on the taller one's shoulder in a comforting manner. "What's wrong?"

Tyler slowly removed his hands from his mouth. The tears were now flowing down his face, a few staining his shirt. Once his hands were at his side, he said three words. Words Felix had partially expected to hear but not said with confidence.

…

…

…

…

"You're not Ryan."

C H A P T E R   S E V E N:

Ryan's Antagonist
////-----------------------------////

The file itself was not that large, but it wasn't small either. After Ryan printed the file out, he skimmed through the pages as he walked through the halls of the school. The students and staff paid no mind to him as he paced about. He couldn't let anyone see this, especially the one whose name is on the front.

Ryan found an empty classroom and sat down on one of the desks. He opened the file and stared at the picture of Felix. Ryan and Felix looked nothing alike. Why did Ryan feel so threatened by him?

Felix Kyle Strand

Age: 17

Birth Date: July 13, 2001

He was the same age as Ryan and Tyler.

Family: Parents, twin sisters [younger]
Father - Damien Marcus Strand
Mother - Tina Lannie Strand
Twin Sister(s) [younger] - Janice Harvey Strand, Gillian Danielle Strand

Ryan chuckled, seeing the names of Felix's twin sisters.

History ~ His family is originally from Alaska. They moved to the U.K. when he was four and his sisters were two. His mother is a doctor and his father is the owner of a bookstore. He went to Faith Primary School as a child and Calderstones School for junior high. He's currently in St. Margaret's Church of England Academy. The hospital his mother works at currently trades with Nico Global often, so the family is familiar with Zander and his family.

Medical Conditions - Asthma [stems from childhood]

Fears - Claustrophobia [fear of tight spaces], Necrophobia [fear of the dead]

The Necrophobia was interesting. Ryan was basically the walking dead. Felix feared the dead to the point of calling it a phobia, which meant he would have panic attacks and become unreasonable. With his medical condition, Felix could even have an asthma attack.

Hobbies - photography, researching the human body, listening to music

Favourite subjects - Science, History, Spanish

The rest of the pages consisted of his most recent social media posts and Facebook pictures. It also included his last known sighting, social security number, and blood type.

The family comes in contact with Zander every now and then because of medicine trade. If they trade on the same day every month, Zander should've met with them a few times. Ryan put his hand on his chin and hummed in confusion. "If we met… would that scare him off?" He shook his head. "Tyler needs a friend…"

The way Tyler is now… He'd be crushed if Felix suddenly just left him alone. It seemed the blonde understood him. Ryan gripped the paper, wrinkling it slightly. "That won't stop me from checking him out myself."

He looked at the file once more, searching for a cell number. "Royce, you couldn't have given me a phone number, too?" He grumbled.

How could he possibly get his phone number without coming in contact with him? This was supposed to be anonymous. Ryan ran his fingers through his hair. "Maybe…" He whispered softly, "I might have to…" He sighed again.

Looks like he was going to have to steal his brother's phone.

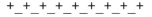

He took his brother's phone when Tyler was called into the hallway by his girlfriend.

It didn't take long for him to figure out his password. It was 1537, a mix of Ryan's age and his favourite numbers. His phone didn't have many people in the contacts. Mother was his speed dial. Felix was the first one on his recent call list.

Ryan made the invite short and simple.

The Aquatics Centre @ five tonight. Don't be late.

He didn't even wait for a reply; he just set the phone back on the desk and left as quick as possible. He didn't want Tyler to notice him. Plus he needed to prepare himself for confronting Felix.

When the time to meet came around, Ryan stood in front of the Aquatics Centre filled with anticipation. He waited by the door with his hands in his pockets. His breath turned visible in the cold air. A white coloured car pulled up in the almost empty parking lot. The teenager Ryan was waiting for exited the car and walked up to him. "Tyler, are you alright after that panic attack earlier today?" Felix asked, walking up to Ryan. His features twisted in confusion, now noticing that though it was the same face, it wasn't the twin he was familiar with. "Ty...ler?"

Ryan walked closer to Felix, now standing three feet away from him. "No," he said, "I'm not Tyler."

Felix took a step back. "Then…"

"My name is Ryan."

The blonde's eyes widened in realization. "W...what?"

"I am Ryan Godfrey, Tyler Godfrey's younger brother," then he added out of habit, "by three minutes."

He was silent for a minute. The question that was burning brightly in his mind at that moment was simply, "... Aren't you dead?" His voice was quiet. "He said you were dead." He was shaking. "Am I dead? I-is that why I can see you?"

Ryan ignored the symptoms brought on by his phobia. "I just want to ask you a few questions," he said, trying to keep the blonde calm.

"You're supposed to be dead!!" he shouted. Felix ran his fingers through his hair before pulling on it. "He said you were dead!!" He kneeled on the ground, pointing at Ryan with a shaking hand.

"Mr. Strand, please stand up." Ryan knew what was going to happen. "I just want to ask you some questions about my brother." He just needed a few more minutes. "Can you tell me how long you've known Tyler?"

Felix's breathing was rushed. "S-shut up!!" He began to shake his head repeatedly, whispering the phrase, 'not real' to himself over and over again. "Shut up!!" He thought he was hallucinating. "You're not real!!" It seemed he thought Ryan was a ghost. "Y-you're not real…" He let out a sigh and collapsed on the ground, hyperventilating.

Ryan smiled. This was going according to plan. All that was left was to transport him to someplace where he can't run. Ryan looked around the parking lot. There weren't many hotels around, but maybe he could find someplace that wouldn't pay any mind to a corpse-like figure crashing at their business.

Now, the task at hand. He wasn't exactly strong - so how was he going to move Felix's body into the car and then into the motel?

He sighed. He'll just have to deal with it.

Felix opened his eyes to the same thing he encountered when he closed them. It was dark. He heard fabric rustle and the click of a lightswitch. When a dim light devoured the room, Felix was met with a pair of green eyes and Tyler's face. "Tyler?" he asked, unsure.

The teen sighed. "We've been over this, Mr. Strand. I am Ryan. Ryan Godfrey."

It took a few moments for the blonde to process what was being said. "Aren't… aren't you dead?" Felix studied Ryan, a confused look painted on his features.

"Do I look dead?" Ryan asked.

Ryan took the silence-filled air as his answer. Ryan stood up from his chair and stretched his arms above his head. "I asked you to meet with me at the

Aquatics Centre a few hours ago. You had a panic attack and fainted."

Felix looked around the motel room. "And you brought me here..?"

Ryan nodded. "This is just a precaution. I could've left you there, but I needed a place that's not easily escapable."

"What?" It was then Felix noticed the folder in his hand. "What's that?" He asked, pointing to it.

"I had a friend give me all the information they could find on you. That's how I knew about your phobias, thus taking advantage of them. It also includes everything about your family, interactions, everyday schedules, etc." He set the folder on the chair behind him. "As I said before you fainted, I want to ask you a few questions about my brother."

The blonde was visibly shaking and his breathing was loud. "About Tyler?"

"Please calm down," He saw that his condition was getting worse. "We can't have you fainting again."

Felix put his index finger and middle finger on the vein most visible on his forearm. "Okay…" he said, breathing in and out deeply. "Okay…" He shut his eyes and nodded towards Ryan. "A-ask away…"

Ryan sat on the bed and pulled out a voice recorder and a small notepad. After pressing the button to record, He began to ask his questions. "How long have you known my brother?"

The blonde gulped. "T-two months... Why is th-"

"You wouldn't understand." Ryan cleared his throat. "What's your relation to Zander White?"

"D-don't you have that in the file?"

Ryan nodded. "I just need you to confirm it."

The blonde teen struggled to speak. "My m-mother works at a hospital and they trade with... Zander himself comes in every once in awhile. Sometimes he brings his daughter N-Nicole... My family is very acquainted   with them because of this. Um..." Felix stared at Ryan, mentally asking if that was enough information. "I-is that all?" He asked, unsure.

Ryan nodded. "How long have you known him?"

"Zander?" He opened his eyes and looked at the lamp next to him. "Uh... maybe two years..."

He nodded again. "What are your thoughts about Tyler's mental state?'

Felix raised his eyebrow. "M-mental state?"

"Yes. I know you brought him to the school's infirmary when he fainted a while back. I also know he vented to you about me. What'd you think about him?"

At first, the blonde shrugged. It was indeed an odd question, but Ryan felt it needed to be asked. "U-uh, he seemed to think he was guilty of your d-death."

Ryan stopped writing. "Guilty…?"

"Y-yeah, he said something about you still being alive if he made it to the rooftop in time. Did you really jump-"

He stopped writing and sighed. "Liar."

"W-what…?"

The brown-haired teen rushed over to Felix, grabbing his collar and yanking his body upwards. "You're a liar!!" He shouted, clearly intoxicated with rage and fury. "Stop lying to me!!" He pulled a cassette tape from his back pocket and showed it to him. "That's not what he said at all."

Felix stared at him, confused. "I-I don't understand…" He said.

"I know his exact words!! Your exact words!! Don't lie to me; I'll know!!" Ryan threw the cassette tape to the other side of the room. "How'd you know about that!? How?!"

The blonde had a frightened look on his face. His eyes were wide, his breathing was quick and shallow, and he looked as if he were on the verge of tears. "I-I, um…"

"Tell me!!"

"I looked at the article!!"

Ryan let go of his shirt collar. "There were multiple articles written about my death; which one are you referring to?"

"... The one by Benjamin Lane."

"He was one of the detectives investigating my death." And Royce's father.

"Y-yeah. He described it as 'an obvious suicide.'"

"I know. I've read the article." Ryan studied Felix's frightened expression. He needed to wrap this up quickly. "Back to Tyler's mental state. What were your thoughts?"

"Uh," He stuttered, "T-Tyler seems really sensitive about this whole thing. It seems anything can trigger a panic attack."

Ryan wrote the blonde's exact words down in his notebook. He was gathering his things, preparing to leave, but he had one question remaining in his mind. He turned towards Felix, who was also preparing to leave. "Do you value Tyler?" He asked, clearly interested.

"V-value?" The blonde thought for a moment. "He's my friend."

Ryan nodded and left the room. He had successfully evaluated Felix Strand. Now all that was left was to wait and observe; he needed to make sure the blonde didn't do anything drastic while consumed with fear.

The clock was ticking.

C H A P T E R   E I G H T:
Timeline of Cheats
////----------------------------////

TY - I'm waiting at the school; text me when you get there

 Why? What's up? - Ry

Ty - Melissa wants us to help her practice for her performance next week

 I forgot she was accepted into that dance school. Can we really help her though? - Ry

Ty - Dude, just get over here. I don't wanna be alone with her

 Haha, alright. I'll be there in a few minutes - Ry

Ryan put his phone back in his pocket and began to walk towards the school's back entrance. He had spent most of his time on the soccer field nowadays to study since the exams were coming close. He walked slowly, letting his bare feet sink into the wet grass. He felt his phone vibrate in his pocket. He chuckled. "Impatient as ever…"

Once he had arrived at in the school's gymnasium, he began to look for his brother. "Tyler!! He called out, listening to his voice echo throughout the empty gym. "Tyler!" He said again. He heard the tap of footsteps behind him. Ryan turned around to look at the owner of the steps. "Hi Melissa," Ryan whispered, "Where's Tyler?"

She pulled a phone out of her vest pocket. The case had a mixture of music notes on it of all different colours. "Tyler actually went home a while ago. I swiped this from his bag." Melissa tossed the phone behind her and took three steps forward. "I'm bored, Youngest…" She smiled as she pushed him up against the wall. "Entertain me, won't you?"

It was the same thing every few days. When it was just the two of them, she'd simply say 'entertain me' and his mind would go blank. He knew what he was doing was wrong, but the part of him that reacted to seduction wouldn't listen.

He was pushed up against the wall, a part of him attempting to push Melissa away and the other pulling her close. "Melissa," He huffed out once he managed to push her away, "The bell is going to ring soon…"

She hugged him tightly, biting his neck once close enough. "And?"

The faint creak of a door was heard behind them, but she ignored the sound and bit Ryan's neck hard enough to leave a mark. Once she heard him wince, Melissa released his neck and stepped back. "I'm going to head to my next class, Youngest. I'll see ya later." She said as she waved him off.

Ryan leaned against the wall and sighed, rubbing the bite mark on his neck. Why couldn't he put a stop this?

"You're Godfrey, aren't you?" a female voice said. It wasn't Melissa, her voice was louder.

He turned towards the voice. "Yeah…" he said shakily. "You are…?"

"Nicole. That's not your girlfriend, right?" She said pointing towards the direction Melissa went.

A worried look was drawn on Ryan's face. There was no use in hiding it now. "How'd you know?"

Nicole pushed her glasses farther back on her nose and clicked her tongue. "You seem more awkward than your brother. She doesn't hang out with you as much as the other one, so this was a weird surprise."

For a few minutes, neither of the two said anything. "You want to put an end to this?" she asked, gesturing his 'relationship' with Melissa.

Ryan knelt down on the floor and hugged his knees. "Please."

She sat down next to the young teen. "I'll convince her to put a stop to this."

"Really?"

"But there's a price for freedom."

He stared at his shoes and nodded for her to continue. Nicole stretched her arms out above her head. "Become my errand boy."

Ryan turned to her, confused. "That's all?"

She nodded. "That's all I ask."

+_+_+_+_+_+_+_+_+_+

It had gone on for two weeks when Ryan had come to a decision.

He knew this was wrong. He knew it from the start, but he couldn't stop. He never knew why, and he feared he never would. Ryan knew he had to put a stop to it. Ryan invited Nicole to the rooftop during lunch without alerting Tyler of his location. The twins usually ate lunch together, but today Ryan had to cancel without notice. He knew his brother would be confused, but he always respected Ryan's wishes.

Ryan waited for Nicole on the roof as he promised. Nicole never made him do the things Melissa did, but what she did make him do was quite annoying. He was certainly her 'errand boy'. Nicole made him gather papers, be the 'in-between' during fights she had with her friends, and even help her cheat during multiple tests and exams. Not to mention being the 'go between' for her 'friend' so she could get speed for an all-nighter to study.

He heard the door of the rooftop open and close with a clunk. "You wanted to see me, Ryan?"

Nodding, he stood up from his seat on the floor. "Yeah, I want to discuss something important."

"That is-?"

"I want to tell Tyler." She stared at him in confusion at first. Ryan sighed and looked at her, the determined light in his eyes getting stronger. "Everything."

"What?!" She ran to him in anger and confusion. "No!! You can't!!" she huffed. "I-I'll get kicked out of school! That'll ruin my chances of getting into an Ivy League college, and my dad will disown me if he finds out!" She took a deep breath. "No! You can't!"

"And why not?"

"Uh-he, uh." She struggled to speak. "If I tell him," she began, "I can add in lies. I can add in things to make you seem like the bad guy!" She gripped Ryan's shoulders, her nails digging into his arms. "Who do you think he'll believe, you or me?!"

Ryan thought for a moment, gritting his teeth in determination. He trusted his brother, and his brother trusted him. If Tyler was given false information making him seem like the bad guy... who would he believe? In the end, this wasn't a difficult question to answer. So he turned to her, his stare stern.

"Me."

Almost immediately after hearing his answer, Nicole pushed him as hard as she could towards the edge of the roof. He stumbled backwards and tripped on the ledge, falling.

In Nicole's eyes, Ryan fell back slowly, reaching for anyone to pull him from his fate, but in all reality, he fell faster than she could blink. She heard the door of the roof open and close quickly accompanied with a pair of footsteps coming directly towards her.

She turned to the teen next to her and was met with the face shared by the twins. Tyler had his fingers laced in his hair and hot tears streaming down his face. He ran to the ledge and looked down, shouting his brother's name in a ragged cry.

Nicole watched him cry and shout, not yet realizing the warm stream of tears were falling down her cheeks, as well. It took her a few moments before noticing that Tyler had stopped crying for his brother and had begun to scream a string of curses directed towards her.

She covered her eyes and sobbed. She only had one thought her in mind at that moment.

…

…

…

She killed him.

She killed Ryan.

///////++++++++///////

Zander arrived at the hospital at six o'clock that afternoon as he did every month. He was always there for at least an hour and a half every month. It was always the same. He did the same things each time he was there for trade. The orders were always the same. The same drugs and medicines, same equipment, same methods.

The man found all of it so boring. The only fun part was meeting with the Strand family. He usually had other people take care of the personal trades, but Zander liked dealing with this hospital himself. He liked the Strands. It was an intriguing family, though their background was boring. He was extremely interested.

He almost found them more interesting than the youngest Godfrey.

Though Ryan was an interesting one, little does the teen know Zander will always be one step ahead of him.

"Mr. White!" a doctor said, walking over to him. "How good to see you!"

Zander turned to meet them and smiled. "Ah, Dr. Tina. Likewise."

The young woman chuckled, tucking a stack of papers under her arm. "If you'd like, you can even call me 'Dr. Strand', you know."

He grinned. "I'll keep it in mind."

"By the way..." Dr. Strand whispered, scratching the side of her head. "Felix has been asking for you."

"Really? Why?"

"I'm afraid I don't know. You'll have to ask him yourself."

Zander waved goodbye as he walked away to look for the doctor's oldest child. He was acquainted enough to know where the children would dwell this time of day. There was a conference room that was barely ever used, so the Strand children stayed there until their mother was done working or their father came to pick them up.

When the man arrived at the door of the conference room, he knocked on the door. "Hello?" He opened it to find the twins by their lonesome. Putting on a smile, he spoke in a sweet tone, "Hello, girls. Do you know where I can find your brother?"

At first the two shook their heads. "Actually," the oldest, Gillian, said, "He might be in Mom's office."

After he thanked the girls, he left to travel through the twists and turns of the hospital once more. Tina was barely ever in her office, so he thought she had given it up to one of her subordinates. Zander read the nameplate next to the door.

Tina L. Strand

He knocked. "Fe? You in there?" The man heard nothing for a moment. A muffled 'come in' broke the silence. Zander walked in the room and sat in an armchair across the large desk in the corner.

Felix was sitting in his mother's chair, squeezing a small stress ball over and over again. "Hey, Zander," he mumbled softly, now bouncing the foam ball in his hand.

The older man watched the blonde for a few moments, his mind wondering what could be causing this strange behaviour. He cleared his throat. "Your mom said this was important. You mind telling me what's up?"

The teen mumbled something unintelligible.

"What was that, Fe?"

He cleared his throat and spoke loud and clear. "Is it true?"

A confused look painted itself on Zander's face. "Is what true?"

Felix looked at Zander dead in the eyes so the older male could clearly see the fear in his eyes.

"Is R-Ryan…" He gulped loudly. "Is Ryan alive…?"

Zander said nothing. He stared at the blonde, annoyed. He took a deep intake of air, slowly exhaling.

…

…

…

…

"What do you know about him?"

C H A P T E R N I N E:

Anxiety of the Knowing
////------------------------------////

"What do you know about him?"

Felix said nothing. He looked down at his lap, putting the stress ball back on his mother's desk. "Not much…" he whispered, "That's why I asked you." The two sat in silence for a few minutes. Neither could think of anything to say. Zander sighed. "Why don't we start with the basics?"

The teen looked confused. "Basics?"

"How'd you meet him? Where'd this all start?"

The blonde began with the text he received a few days ago. He found it odd, a random text asking to meet like that. Without questioning it, he went to meet Tyler, or the one he thought was Tyler.

He talked about Ryan revealing himself. His panic attack. The 'interrogation' about Tyler.

Felix had almost gotten through the whole story when Zander stopped him. "You left after he did, right? How long after?"

"… about ten minutes."

He nodded. "I can ask Ryan about the rest…" He whispered the rest of his sentence. "I'll get more information out of him anyway." The man cleared his throat and stood up from the chair. "Now, how'd you first hear about Ryan-" He emphasized his last name. "-Godfrey?"

The blonde sat in thought, tapping his fingers on the metal surface of the desk. "I guess when my Mind Sciences class was assigned a date to look up. We were supposed to find some crime, incident or extravaganza that went on. I was assigned the date 'March 2nd, 2015'."

"The day Ryan 'died'."

"Yeah… That's when I began the research. I looked at multiple articles and multiple social media posts dedicated to him."

"There are interviews with his family online, too. Did you look at those?"

Felix hesitated before answering. "... Yeah."

Zander felt the temperature rising in the room. He couldn't tell if he was nervous or they turned the heat on. He took off his sweater and sat down in the same armchair as before. "What did the two of you talk about, Fe?"

"Um…" He struggled to remember what he tried so hard to forget. "He wanted to know how long I've known Tyler and you, but he was most interested with Tyler's mental state…"

"And what'd you say?"

"He is…" The blonde wondered if he should reword the phrase or not. "Sensitive."

"Do you think Tyler knows Ryan is alive?" The older man said, crossing his legs.

Felix shook his head. "No. I'm sure he'd be ecstatic to find out his brother is alive. He doesn't fit that part, so I guess not."

Zander couldn't think of anymore questions. He got up to leave when a certain question was birthed by his brain. "Has Ryan attempted to contact you since this meeting of yours?"

He shook his head again. "Not that I know of."

"Alright." He opened the door and waved goodbye to the teen. Walking down the hallways of the hospital, he was met with a few familiar staff members greeting him with a smile. He returned the smiles, with a fake one, of course. He was set on consulting with Ryan about this. He knew the teen would be shocked to an extent, but Zander wasn't doing this for the satisfaction of annoying the teen. He needed to know his plans and put a stop to them. If needed, he'd have to isolate Ryan to make sure he didn't get out and cause trouble again.

At least then, they might complete the tests faster. "Who knows, Ryan might be happy to get this over with." Zander chuckled as he exited the building.

"… Probably not."

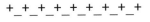

Felix sighed loudly once he was sure Zander was out of earshot. He had worked up anxiety since meeting with Ryan. The stress ball on his mother's desk had kind of helped him, but the way Zander had looked at him with such vexation made the situation worse.

He was aware that Ryan and Tyler were twins, just not identical twins. The way Tyler described him, it just didn't seem likely that the two were identical; Felix thought for sure they were fraternal. Now that he's seen the shared face of the Godfrey twins, he doesn't know how to face Tyler.

His mind is so fragile. Felix knew he felt guilty somehow. Being the son of a doctor, seeing through people's masks was a knack he just so happened to pick up. Tyler thinks Ryan supposedly killing himself was his fault.

The blonde was aware he wasn't the most quiet person there was, and by that he meant he wasn't one to keep a secret. He knows Ryan is alive. How would he face Tyler? The nervousness and stress piling up on him from having to keep such a big secret between him and Nico Global, Felix didn't think he'd last.

Felix would have to distance himself from Tyler until he got himself under control. The blonde wasn't going to be able to keep this secret from Tyler, so he has to make sure they never come in contact with one another.

Unless Tyler knows, too. Zander could've told him. Felix chuckled and shook his head. Not likely. Zander wouldn't do that, would he? If this is such a big secret, he wouldn't tell anyone. He wouldn't want anyone to know, right?

No, this is a big discovery. Bringing people back from the dead? The world has been dreaming of that for years. Zander had figured out how to do it. Why didn't he want people to know? Maybe he wanted people to know, but he doesn't know how he did it? Maybe Zander doesn't know how he brought Ryan back. Is that what he's trying to figure out?

What if that's why he doesn't want Tyler to know? He wants to have a good explanation for the Godfrey family. He wants to know how they did it, so there's a less likely percentage that Ryan's family will sue Zander's company.

Felix tried to remember the characteristics of Ryan on the night they met. He recalled fading scars on his hands and collarbone. A bandage on his forehead, just barely covered by his hair. Where'd those injuries come from? Was Zander taking blood to test what they did?

The teen suddenly felt a sharp pang through his head. He sighed, relaxing his muscles against the soft leather of the chair. This wasn't good for him, to think this much. He needed sleep. He'd think about this tomorrow, but now his mind needed to recalibrate.

Tyler knew he should be at home asleep. The night was dark and cold, two attributes he did not appreciate. Instead, he was at Saint Matthew and St. James Mossley Hill Parish Church. He needed a place to think. The school was too crowded at this time of night, so he couldn't go there. He decided to go to a church, but instead of the one directly next to the school he went to one five minutes away by cycling.

The church was quiet and beautiful. The perfect place to think. God is believed to be closer when you're inside a church, so it's helpful when you're thinking about things such as death. Tyler sat down on the pew and allowed his head to rest in his hands. He thought back to when Ryan was alive. He seemed so happy and independent. The only time he can remember Ryan being sad was around their fifteenth birthday.

Ryan always seemed down and gloomy then. He didn't talk much and he'd disappear whenever Tyler was around. The two stopped eating lunch together. Ryan was nowhere to be found when he went to look for him.

Tyler looked at the stained glass ceiling of the church. "What'd I do, God?" He whispered. "What'd I do?" He leaned back and sighed. He didn't want to believe that Ryan dying was his fault, but he just couldn't push the thought away. It remained in his mind, refusing to dissipate.

He thought back to when he saw Ryan at the Aquatics Centre. He was staring at him, his eyes empty. Those green eyes once full of life were empty. So many thoughts hit him at once and he just couldn't take it anymore. Tyler surrendered to the sleep his mind offered, right of the cold tiled floor of the Aquatics Centre.

When he woke up hours later, he was back at home laying on the couch. His mother was sitting in the armchair nearby reading a book entitled **Bluefish**. At first, the teen said nothing to his mother who hadn't notice he had awakened, but when he finally mustered enough courage to voice the thought on his mind, he was still accompanied with silence.

"I saw Ryan."

He didn't realize what that silence meant at that moment but now he does. Ryan is dead. He knows, his mother knows, Bryan knows. He can't bring him back, but his mind won't give up on it. It kept on saying 'you can bring him back' or 'he's not dead'.

Tyler knows that he can't. During the wake held for Ryan, Tyler touched the corpse of his brother. It was cold. It meant Ryan was gone. The heat of his soul was gone.

Tyler twirled his phone around in his hand. He looked at the ceiling once more, taking in the music of the choir. He began to sing along quietly, thinking and thinking. Finally he decided to ask Ryan the one question that he refused to go unanswered.

"What did I do to make you resort to this, Ryan?"

...

…

…

All he received was silence.

Tyler sighed and gulped down another pill.

C H A P T E R T E N:

The Art of Isolation
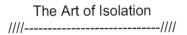

Ryan was on his bed with headphones in his ears, the music blaring while he studied for upcoming tests. He tapped his fingers to the beat and quickly skimmed the pages. Though his music was loud, it couldn't block out the two knocks on his door that he heard. Ryan simply took one earbud off and listened.

"Ryan." It was Zander. He sounded annoyed. "Meet me in my study."

The teen heard footsteps grow farther and farther away. "Crap." Zander found out. Ryan took out his earbuds and shoved his phone away. The book he was using to study fell onto the floor causing the pages to fold every which way.

Ryan ran his fingers through his hair and began to walk to the study. When he arrived in the small room, Zander was sitting at his desk twirling a pen around in his fingers. "You wanted to see me?" Ryan croaked out.

"Yeah." He set the pen down. "I had a chat with the Strand family's oldest earlier today. You know him - Felix?"

The teen grit his teeth and inhaled sharply. "What about him?" he asked.

"Oh no, nothing about him. I'm just curious about how he thought to ask me if it was true that *Ryan* was alive." Zander stared at the teen, his eyes stern. "How'd he know about you, Ryan? I mean, he's a friend of your brother, but how would he know about your being alive?"

Ryan said nothing. His fingers curled in anticipation. There was a catch to this. He was playing dumb for a reason. "You already know don't you, Zander?" he said, "Stop feigning innocence." The teen saw a smirk grow on the man's face.

"You've been watching your brother, haven't you? That's how you knew about Felix." All Zander received was silence. "I'll take that as a 'yes'." The smirk he wore evolved into a grin. "Ryan, I've decided something."

The teen stared at the wooden tiles of the study, his gloomy expression blocked by the hair that had fallen onto his face. "What is that?"

"I'm relocating you a private facility of Nico Global where we can continue to test every possible formula to figure out how we resurrected you. The facility is on the coast of California; I'll be visiting often to check on progress. You'll be moved there in exactly one week by aircraft, that should give you more than enough time to pack your things." The man pointed to the door. "Leave." His smile fell. "I'll explain the rest to you tomorrow morning."

Ryan nodded. "Yes, sir." The teen left the room without another word.

He walked to his room in silence, his footsteps echoing throughout the empty hallway. His room was lit by a small lamp on his desk. The small bedroom was practically empty. He had a few books on the bookshelf, a computer complete with other wires, and photos of his family. Ryan stared at his computer, a light going off in his head.

He ran to his swivel chair, quickly sitting down and opened his laptop. Ryan composed an email about his relocation to isolation. Before he pressed send, he typed a simple word into the subject line.

{URGENT}

Then he clicked send, whispering one sentence before calling it a night. "Please help me, Royce."

Tyler didn't remember seeing anyone put a sticky note on his desk; it must've been when he stepped out to speak to the teacher about exam week and down another pill. The handwriting on the note looked vaguely familiar, but Tyler paid no mind to it. He looked around the almost empty classroom to see if anyone seemed to know where the note came from. He skimmed it, looking for the name of the sender. When he found none, he decided to read it.

You most likely don't know who I am, but I know who you are. I know about your brother's death. I have some information on him that I think you deserve to know. Meet me by the bleachers on the left side of the soccer field. I'm wearing a bright red shirt and white sunglasses. Please get here as quick as you can.

Tyler read the note several times before the message sunk in. Someone knew something about Ryan. Tyler didn't know who this was from; it could be anyone. Was it Felix? Tyler hadn't seen him in awhile. The note asked him to get there as quick as he could, was it that urgent? He didn't know if he should trust it.

Sighing, Tyler began to make his way towards the soccer field. When he arrived by the bleachers, he noticed a few people had begun to gather to watch the team prepare for the upcoming game. Just as the note said, the composer was wearing a bright red t-shirt and white sunglasses. He was sitting on the top bench of the rusted bleachers.

Tyler walked up the steps, studying the teen as he stepped closer. He sat down next to the guy, placing his hands on his lap. The two sat in silence for a moment before he began to speak. "When I tell you what I know, I need you to promise me one thing."

Tyler looked at him in confusion. "What's that?"

"... Don't freak out." When the teen had the confirmation from Tyler, he spoke. "I was born on February 28th of the year 2000. I'm of a pair of twins; I am the younger brother by three minutes." Not noticing how the information, this supposedly unrelated information concerning Ryan, was adding up, Tyler gestured for him to continue.

"My mother's name is Charlotte Evelynn Kim and my father's name is Daniel Noel Godfrey, but my parents are divorced. My step-dad is Bryan Steven Shepard."

When Tyler heard his family's names, he put his hand over the teen's mouth thus silencing him. "That's my parents' names." The teen nodded. "How're they your parents as well?"

He moved Tyler's hand. "You didn't let me finish." He took a deep breath. "I still need to tell you my name." He looked at Tyler noticing how wide his eyes were. "My name..." He gulped, taking off the sunglasses. "My name is Ryan."

There was a silence between them that seemed to have lasted a lifetime, but in all reality, it only lasted a few seconds before Tyler began to chuckle loudly. A shocked look found its way onto Ryan's facial features. He didn't expect his brother to laugh after hearing this shocking truth.

"Ah, I must be hallucinating again," he said once his laughter died down, "I'm sorry, you're going to have to repeat that. I'm afraid my ears heard something impractical."

"You believe you're hallucinating, Tyler?"

Tyler chuckled once more. "Yeah... I mean, ever since my..." He stopped. "Who am I kidding? Maybe it's because our birthday was a little while ago, but I see him everywhere. I know he's dead." He cleared his throat as if to retract his previous sentence. "A part of me knows he's dead, but the other part doesn't wish to accept it."

"... That part of you that believes your brother is dead," the one claiming to be Ryan said, looking to see if Tyler was paying attention, "What does it think about my saying I'm Ryan?"

Tyler shrugged and began to fiddle with the hem of his sweatshirt. "... I want to believe you."

"... But?"

Tyler felt tears begin to form at the corners of his eyes. He turned to look at the one claiming to be Ryan. "He died." Tyler gulped. "... *You* died." He felt the tears he had tried to eliminate fall down his face. "R-Ryan…?" Tyler reached for his brother, but as his hand grew closer to his brother, he stopped.

It was like Ryan could read his thoughts.

"I'm not going to disappear."

Tyler threw his arms around his brother just as quick as he disregarded the onlookers. At that point he didn't care; he was just happy he had his brother back.

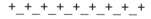

They moved from the bleachers to the gym storage room. Ryan felt if they were outside for much longer they'd attract too much attention. The younger brother stared at Tyler, noticing the facial features they shared had grown slightly different. Though they had the same face, Tyler had freckles on his nose and cheeks, and Ryan had a small mole under his left eye. He noticed how his brother's face was stained with tears, causing his cheeks to redden.

The two of them had once shared similar characteristics. Ryan and Tyler used to hold the same amount of strength to protect one another or their friends. The same amount of courage, patience, humility, devotion, etc. Ryan failed to notice that as time went on Tyler had begun to lose his courage and strength.

It made his older brother seem fragile compared to him.

Ryan had seen how the world works, the way people can be corrupted by greed of money and material items. It helped him grow in terms of experience and wisdom. When Ryan died, the things that had made Tyler who he was as a twin just disappeared. Ryan couldn't help but feel it was his fault.

Tyler noticed his brother's uneasiness and attempted to comfort him. "Don't think too much, Ry."

The younger one looked at his brother, now fully appreciating the gentleness he was gifted with. Ryan imagined this being how he could comfort him when he confessed to him the things he's done. Though a part of him believed he wouldn't comfort him at all.

"Hey… Tyler," he said finally, "Won't you run away with me?"

C H A P T E R   E L E V E N:
Run Away with the Runaway
////-----------------------------////

All the emotions Tyler was feeling at that moment were clearly painted onto his face. The main one he was feeling though was confusion. Tyler tilted his head to the side. "W-what do you mean 'run away'?" he asked quietly.

His brother sighed, resting the palm of his hand on his knee. "I'll explain everything later, Tyler, but right now I need an answer. I don't have much time before he figures out where I ran off to."

Tyler wanted to ask about so many things, but he kept his mouth shut. Taking a deep breath, he stared at his brother, his eyes filled with determination. He trusted Ryan. "Okay," he said, "Let me grab some things from the house." He smiled at his brother. "Then you can lead the way."

Ryan escorted Tyler to the car he used to drive to school. They drove back to Tyler's home and parked a few streets away. "I'll wait in the car," Ryan said, tapping his fingers on the steering wheel, "Go get the necessities for a few days and nights."

The older brother nodded while exiting the car. He waved as he ran to their house, kicking up dust as he did so. Tyler noticed his mother's car wasn't in the driveway. It made him sigh in relief. Tyler rushed up to his room, gathering what he could before rushing back out.

He heard the quiet clashing of dishes in the kitchen as he stepped down the stairs. His foot hit a hollow spot on the wooden stairs causing a loud creak to echo through the house. Tyler heard the clashing of dinner plates stop. "Tyler?" He heard his mother shout. "Is that you?"

Sighing, the teen put on a smile and walked into the kitchen to greet his mother. "Hello, Ma," he said, waving, "When did you get home?"

"I've been here, dear. Bryan went to take my car to the shop." She set the dishes by the sink. "How long have you been here, mister?" she said, placing her hands on her hips.

Tyler turned to the front door, peering through the small window. Ryan's still waiting for him, so he needed to make this conversation with his mother quick. "Ma, I've just come home to grab some stuff for an overnight trip."

"An overnight trip? With whom? Where?"

"Um…" Tyler fiddled with his fingers. "With Felix. I'm going over to his house for the night… He's waiting for me outside, so I've got to get going."

His mother smiled. "He's outside? How about I go say 'hi'?" she said, beginning to walk towards the door.

Tyler waved his hands frantically. "Mom! No! I've got to get going, okay?" He hugged his mother. "I love you, and I'll see you later!" He ran towards the door, quickly opening it and exiting. He saw his mother awkwardly wave goodbye to him .

He knew his mother was suspicious, but he couldn't bother with it right now. His brother needed him. Tyler saw his brother's car still waiting by an unknown neighbour's house. Once he believed he was far away enough from his home, he began to walk towards the silver Ford Fiesta. "Ryan…" he huffed once in the car. "Can you tell me what this is about now?"

His brother just shook his head. "We need to get farther away before I can say anything." Ryan turned to Tyler, noticing the distraught expression upon him. He sighed. "I promise, I'll tell you everything later, but right now… We just need to leave."

Tyler nodded, though he wasn't sure as to what was going on. He took a deep breath, listening to the rumble of the engine. His last thought before slipping into the land of dreams was… 'Could he really trust this resurrected Ryan?'

Ryan watched as his brother was lulled to sleep by the car. After an hour of driving in circles, he stopped at a local diner to enter the address of Royce's safehouse into the GPS. His brother stirred a small bit as the car pulled to a stop. Once Ryan had put the address in, he stepped out of the car and pulled out his cell phone.

He glanced at the address, Delamere Forest, Frodsham, once more before throwing his phone onto the concrete pavement and crushing it with his foot. "I can't let Zander track my phone's GPS…" he whispered, getting back into the driver's seat.

Tyler made a small noise of discomfort in his seat as Ryan buckled his seatbelt. The younger brother peered over at him, checking to see if he was alright. Once the mewls of discomfort faded, Ryan began the drive to Delamere Forest. As he pulled out of the diner parking lot, he realized he'd have to dispose of Tyler's cell phone as well.

That was if Zander thought to track it.

No, Zander wouldn't do that. He'd have to go through hoops in order to have access to Tyler's phone. He'd hate having to do that much work for just a location.

Assured he wouldn't attempt to, Ryan turned on the radio to some random station to keep sound flowing through his ears. He figured the two should get to the forest by nightfall, considering it was nearly four now. The drive would take about an hour, so he could let his brother sleep until they got there.

Ryan sighed as he turned onto the next street. He felt bad about making Tyler leave their mother alone, but he figured Bryan would take care of her. The teen stopped the car in the middle of an empty road. "Mother will be wondering where Tyler is…" Ryan whispered.

He glanced at his brother, scanning for a phone. When he didn't see one with the naked eye, he decided to check his bag. In there, he found his brother's phone with the same music note covered cell phone case. He decided to text the antagonist.

I'm going to be gone for a little while, Felix. Tell my mother, please. Also, make sure she doesn't tell anyone else. This is important to me, but I promise I'll be back in a few days.

Ryan felt he needed to add more so they wouldn't come looking for Tyler. Before sending the message, he added something he knew would make it so his mother wouldn't question Tyler's whereabouts.

Tell her that I need some time with my brother.

The teen began to drive again, but instead of putting Tyler's phone back in his bag, he threw it out the passenger window. Now Zander can't track it if he tried. Ryan was determined to keep his brother safe, through any means necessary.

CHAPTER TWELVE:
The Keeper of the Keys
////-----------------------------////

Ryan pulled into the makeshift driveway of the cabin. There were no lights on in the cabin, no sign that someone was inside. He turned to look at the person in the passenger seat. His brother was asleep, his head against the window. Taking the key out of the ignition, Ryan shook his brother's shoulders to wake him. He made a small noise and opened his eyes. "R-Ryan?"

The teen nodded. "Yeah, Ty, it's me." He pulled an umbrella out from under the seat. "C'mon, get up. We're at the house." Ryan helped his brother out of the car, holding the umbrella above the both of them. As they walked towards the cabin, Tyler would sometimes walk too fast or fall behind his brother by a few steps, causing rain to tumble down on his shoulders and legs. Ryan watched as his brother tripped every few seconds. Since Tyler had just woken up, Ryan assumed it was because of that.

They arrived at the front door, stomping the mud and excess dirt off their shoes. Tyler went to knock, but the door had swung open and a hand pulled the two of them inside. When the two reoriented themselves, they looked at the person who yanked them inside.

The girl was about their age. Her hair was a light chestnut colour. The pale green glasses that rested on the bridge of her nose were slowly sliding down, allowing Ryan to see her grey eyes. "Were you followed?" She asked. Ryan noticed how skinny she was; she was huffing as if she had run over to the door.

Tyler shrugged and looked at his brother. Ryan shook his head slowly and unsure. The two watched as the girl sighed and shook her head in disbelief. She ran her fingers through her hair. "You should've been looking at your mirror, Ryan. Who knows who could have been following you?"

The older twin tilted his head to the side in confusion. The younger one copied. "I'm sorry…" Tyler scratched his head with his index finger. "Who are you?" He pointed at the female teen in front of him.

She shook her head, annoyed. "How do you not know who I am? I mean…" She looked at Tyler, "I understand if you don't know who I am, but, *Ryan*, how do you not know who I am?"

Ryan shook his head, his brown hair falling over his left eye. "I… don't know who you are…"

The female groaned, annoyed once more. She pointed to a framed letter on the wall. "We sent letters back and forth when you were in that facility."

Ryan looked at the letter that was in small print and nailed onto the wall in a wooden frame. The letter wasn't typed, it was written in an orange ink pen. It took a few seconds for Ryan to realize it was his handwriting from when he was 16. He looked back at the girl, squinting his eyes.

"Royce…?"

The teen Ryan called 'Royce' began to clap slowly. "Good job, you know my name; now we need to get to the task at hand." She pointed to the table in the kitchen behind her with her thumb. "Sit. I'll get drinks then we can talk."

The two walked over to the triangle shape birch-wood table and sat on two of the four bar stools surrounding it. Tyler peered over at his brother in confusion. That's right, Ryan hadn't told him about Royce, yet. Ryan leaned closer to his brother. "A little while after I woke up from the fall, I received letters from Royce. We were like pen pals. We grew close over the little bits of info we gave each other every week." Tyler nodded; Ryan continued, "I...." He cleared his throat. "...never knew Royce was a female until today."

A small smile made its way onto Tyler's features. The teen nodded once more and turned to face Royce as she set two cups of tea in front of them. "Hello, Royce," Tyler said, "I'm the older brother, Tyler."

She smiled. "I can tell. You two have the same face after all. And if you think about it, Ryan actually has a fraternal personality to your identical twins." Royce chucked as Ryan scrunched his nose in annoyance. "The thing that is absolutely identical about you two is your care for one another."

Ryan let his forehead hit the table as he slouched and sighed. "Where are you going with this, Royce..."

The smirk she wore grew larger. She leaned close to Ryan's ear. "How about I tell your brother about how you've been spying on him through his phone and computer?"

"Don't you dare!" He whispered angrily. "Don't freak him out!"

"What are you two whispering about?" Tyler said, leaning closer to the two of them. "Should I leave so you two can speak privately?"

Ryan shook his head, chuckling awkwardly. "Of course not, Ty. Royce just wanted to tell me something-"

"Actually, I wanted to inform you, Tyler, that your brother has been spying on you through your cell phone and any other electrical device you have. He was very worried and very snoopy."

Tyler's mouth formed an 'o' shape and his eyes widened. "Is this true, Ryan? You… spied on me?" Ryan sighed loudly and nodded. Tyler gave a half-smile. "You were worried about me, huh… You went through spying on me to make sure I was alright?"

"Yeah…" Ryan ran his fingers through his hair. "I wanted to make sure you were alright. You have been the victim of a few panic attacks lately."

He chuckled. "Oh, you saw those…"

Royce sat across from them. "What triggers your panic attacks, Tyler?"

Ryan turned towards the girl. "You don't ask someone that, Royce, it's rude!"

"Is it rude or embarrassing for your brother?" She said smirking at Ryan.

He sighed and turned towards his brother. "What do you think caused your panic attacks?" Ryan watched as his brother fiddled with his fingers. "What was it, Ty?"

Tyler set his head on the table and sighed. "They started happening more and more around our birthday, Ry. Nothing was as much fun without you then." Royce looked at Ryan, glaring; Tyler continued. "When I met Felix, I didn't connect your likeness until he called me 'Ty'. That triggered the attack at the Aquatics Centre."

Royce tapped her fingers on the table. "Felix Strand?" She turned to Ryan, another smirk plastered on her face with sharp eyes. "Isn't that the person you personally investigated, Ryan? You probably scared him away from your brother!"

Ryan's brother lifted his head up. "Is that the reason he's been avoiding me lately, Ry? You scared him?" Tyler looked at his brother and sighed. "Royce, where will we be sleeping?"

She pointed to the stairs. "Upstairs, it's the room at the end of the hall when you turn left."

He stood up and walked two steps away from the table. "We'll talk about this later, Ryan."

Royce chuckled as the older brother walked upstairs. "I did not expect him to get so pissed about that, Ryan, I'm sorry. Really, I am."

He turned to the girl, an annoyed expression on his face. "What the hell, Royce, why?"

"I said I was sorry, Godfrey." Royce studied the annoyed expression he wore. "Don't tell me you were planning to keep that from him forever. He has to know, and it's better to tell him straight-up so your punishment isn't as bad."

"What's that supposed to mean…"

"He's mad at you, yes, but he won't be for long. You can't keep him in tho dark forever, man." She began to mess with a strand of hair in front of Ryan's eyes. "I know you. You're going to end up doing something that will make him really mad at you." She thought for a moment. "You're going to take his place, aren't you?"

Ryan said nothing as he knew Royce already knew the answer.

"What are you going to do, Godfrey? Lock him in my house? I won't allow that; my father won't allow that."

"I'm not letting Tyler get hurt because of me. I don't know what I'm going to do, but I'm not letting him go home while Zander is still after me."

At first, she said nothing. Royce looked at Ryan's fingers, his knuckles turning white from tightly gripping his hair. "I have sleeping pills in my bathroom cabinet."

He turned to the girl, his eyes wide. "W-what?"

"You can bring him a drink when you go apologize to him; I'll crush up the pills and sprinkle them in it. I don't know how long he'll sleep for, but..."

"Royce?"

"While he's asleep, you go and negotiate a deal of some sort with Zander." She poked his forehead. "Make him give you your life back. Tell him to leave your brother and parents alone." Royce slid a glass coffee cup towards him. "What's his favourite drink?"

Ryan looked at the cup skeptically. Looking back at the girl, he tapped his fingers on the table and sighed. "Orange juice."

Tyler heard a soft knock on the door, causing his head to shoot up in surprise. The door creaked open and in walked Ryan. "Hey," he said, "I brought you a drink." He held in his hand a glass filled with an orange liquid. Tyler said nothing as his brother sat on the bed next to him, setting the cup on the bedside table.

Tyler turned to Ryan. "I've been lonely, y'know?" he said, "I don't have many friends, and Melissa isn't even someone I connect with anymore. Felix helped. I wasn't as lonely."

Ryan looked at his lap in guilt.

"After a while, I thought I was replacing you with him, but then I realized something." Tyler leaned over his brother and grabbed the drink off the bedside table. Taking a sip, he turned back to his brother. "There's nobody out there who can replace you in the memories we share." He chuckled. "Plus, who else has the same face me?"

Ryan felt the guilt he held grow heavier. "Hey, Ty… I-I'm sorry." He watched as his older brother took another large drink of the orange juice. "I'm going to get my life back."

Tyler set the cup between his legs. "What do you mean?"

"I going to find a way for me to get back into the real world. Y'know, live with you and Bryan and Mother again."

"How are you going to do that, Ry?"

He said nothing. Ryan laced his fingers together and sighed, watching his brother take another sip of the drink. "I'm going to meet with Zander tonight." Ryan stood up from the bed and began to walk out of the room, ignoring his brother's questions. "You're staying here."

Tyler went to get out of the bed but immediately fell back onto it. He groaned and held his head. "R-Ryan?" He looked up at his brother, who had opened the door.

"You're going to stay here, Ty," He said.

Tyler saw the guilt on his brother's face before his body surrendered to the drug. "Ry.. an…" The only thing he remembered before blacking out was reaching for his brother, but Ryan didn't grab his hand. He walked out. He left. Tyler couldn't do anything about it.

C H A P T E R   T H I R T E E N:
A System Leak
////-----------------------------////

Felix received the text from Tyler around four that afternoon. He saw the notification. When he gathered the courage to finally read it, he was honestly shocked. Felix knew he hadn't seen Tyler in a few days since he was purposefully avoiding him. Tyler had disappeared during that time, and all he had done to tell his friends and family where he was going was a text. A very cryptic text.

Felix was avoiding Tyler, he freely admits to that. How could he possibly face him when he knows the truth about his supposedly dead brother? That text made everything he thought about the situation burn up. Tyler was fragile, sensitive. When he says he needed to spend time with his brother, that brings up a whole pie chart of possibilities. The first thing that came to his mind and probably his parents', as well, was suicide. At first glance, Tyler didn't seem to be the type of person to contemplate such a thing, but as you get to know him, you tend to think otherwise.

The blonde was at his mother's work, in the conference room with his sisters, as his mother was working late. While his siblings were doing homework, he was reading the text Tyler sent over and over again trying to get some deeper meaning out of it. While he was reading it, he heard the door open. Felix looked up. "Hey, Fe," Zander said as he walked in, "What's up? You look kind of listless."

Felix wasn't even paying attention to the fact that Ryan was a secret anymore. He just wanted answers. "What does Tyler mean when he says he wants to spend time with his brother, Zander?" he asked, still listless. "He wouldn't know Ryan's alive, right?" he whispered.

When his mind returned to the present, he noticed Zander had stopped with the fake smiles and tones. He just stared at the blonde with a very confused and angry look. "What are you talking about, Felix?" Zander saw he had his phone in his hand. Grabbing it, he quickly read the text.

Zander slowly set the phone down. He looked at Felix, whose eyes were wide with fear. "It's not Tyler who sent this text, Fe." He said, in a sing-song tone. Zander slid the phone across the conference table back to Felix. "Take a wild guess on the real writer."

||+++++++++++||

Three men in blue jumpsuits walked with Zander and Felix to an empty road. On the left side of the road was a small diner while on the right there was a sketchy car dealer. Zander pulled out an IPad. After staring at it for a moment, he looked at the diner. He snapped and the three men grabbed hold of Felix's arm and walked towards the entrance of the small restaurant. Zander followed, stopping when they arrived in the parking lot. They found a crushed cellphone. Next, Zander walked into the street.

He picked up a horribly cracked cell phone with a case covered in music notes. He smiled, looking at the road once more. "The forest," He said, laughing, "The twins are in the forest."

||++++++++++||

Ryan sat with Royce at her triangle-shaped table once more. While contemplating how they were going to get in touch with Zander, the two of were sharing a small plate of crackers and cheese. Ryan was nervously tapping his fingers on the table. Royce grabbed his hand, stopping the noise. "Calm down," she said, "I'm sure we'll think of something, and when we do, we'll clear things up with your brother." She cleared her throat. "You'll clear things up with your brother. You'll be with your family again."

Ryan nodded, sighing deeply. "I can't just use your phone, Royce. He'll come here, and he might hurt you or Tylor."

Royce smirked playfully. "You're worried about me, Godfrey? That's sweet, but we've got other things to worry about-"

Suddenly a loud ring echoed through the room.

She walked over to the cabin's phone. She picked it up and answered it. "Hello, Lane residence." Royce said nothing for a moment or two as if she was listening to the person speaking. "Hey, Ryan?" She turned to him. "He's asking for you." Royce handed him the phone. "Here."

Ryan held the phone up to his ear. "Hel..lo?" he asked, confused.

"Hello, Ryan."

He knew that voice. It's the same one he heard after waking up from falling off a building. Ryan turned to Royce, who had sat down next to him, and mouthed the word 'Zander'. Royce nodded and mouthed back 'I know'. "What a coincidence," Ryan said, paying attention to the phone, "I needed to speak with you."

Ryan heard Zander chuckle on the other end. "Likewise."

"I want to meet up with you. I'm sure you know I'm in the forest; let's meet up at the entrance."

"Alright." For a moment, he was quiet. "I'll be waiting. I expect you to be there in twenty minutes or less. Come alone, unarmed."

Ryan sighed. "Okay, I'll be there." Zander hung up and Ryan set the phone down on the table. "Royce, do you mind if I use your dad's old motorcycle to go meet Zander?"

She nodded. "I'll go get the keys."

The girl left the room and disappeared into her father's study. Ryan watched as the door closed. He held his head in his hands, sighing and glancing at the stairwell. When Ryan had left the bedroom he and Tyler were staying in, he saw Tyler reach out to him as if he were hoping that it wasn't real. Tyler wanted it not to be true. That Ryan was leaving him again. He couldn't risk Tyler coming with him.

Ryan heard the light clang of metal from Benjamin Lane's study. He felt guilty, drugging Tyler like that. Suddenly, Royce walked out of the study. "Sorry for the wait, Godfrey. I forgot where my dad put them." She looked at the saddened expression Ryan wore. "Everything's going to be fine. Sort things out with Zander. Tyler will be here when you get back."

He nodded and sighed. Ryan looked at Royce's hand holding the keys to the motorcycle. Taking the keys, he got up from the table and walked into the garage. "If Tyler wakes up," he said, "Tell him I'll be back."

Ryan didn't wait for an answer. He just walked out. He was going to meet Zander, and he was going to settle things.

||++++++++++||

Zander heard the sound of the motorcycle engine twelve minutes after he called Ryan. After the teen stopped the bike, he slowly got off and walked towards Zander and his men. "I'm prepared to hear your proposition, Ryan," He said loudly. The scientist stepped towards the young Godfrey.

Ryan inhaled deeply. "I want to go back home."

"I said soon. I told you already-"

"'You're close'. Yeah, yeah, I know. I don't care if you're close to recreating whatever it is you were attempting to do with all the other corpses, I want to go back home. I want my life back!" His voice was gradually rising in volume. "I wish to go back with my family!!"

Ryan was huffing at the end of his outburst. Zander sighed with annoyance laced in his breath. "Ryan…" The man muttered, "Can't you give me more time?"

The teen's head shook violently. "No! I refuse to stay as your test subject any longer!" Ryan could faintly hear the stomp of feet against the dry ground. Ignoring it, he continued to speak. "I will give you some of my blood to continue experimenting with, but I refuse to stay in the custody of you and Nico Global."

Ryan watched the cloud of confliction invade Zander's eyes. The man was thinking, but Ryan couldn't yet tell what his final decision would be. Finally, he spoke: "No."

"W-what?"

"No. It's as simple as that." Zander turned to the few men that accompanied him. "Shoot him."

The teen's eyes widened. "W-what?!"

Suddenly, the sound of feet hitting the ground grew closer and Ryan saw his brother invade his eyesight and push him away. "Zander!!" Tyler shouted. "Leave Tyler alone!!"

A confused look appeared on Ryan's face. At first, he didn't know what he was doing, but then realization hit him

...

...

…

He was going to take his place.

CHAPTER FOURTEEN:
An Unlucky Gamble
////----------------------------////

Tyler awoke with a start. He rolled off the mattress and onto the floor. He quickly stood up and rushed into the room's connecting bathroom, violenting vomiting into the toilet. He threw up all those pills he'd taken and whatever Ryan put in his drink.

He sat on the ground next to the vomit-filled toilet, recalling what Ryan said before he left, what he said he was doing. Tyler stood, leaning on the wall as he walked down the stairs, startling Royce who sat alone at the kitchen table.

"Where's Ryan?" He croaked out. "Where'd my brother go?"

At first, Royce said nothing. She sighed. "Just follow the road."

And, with that, Tyler left. He walked, following the road as Royce instructed. The unpaved road was filled with twists and turns, and through the trees, Tyler could see headlights. He decided to forgo the road and strutted through the path between the trees.

When he was close enough, Tyler was going to say something, he didn't know what, but that's what he was going to do. All he heard when he was close enough though, was 'shoot him'.

Needless to say, he acted without thinking.

Ryan watched as Tyler flew in front of him, pushing him backward with one of his arms. "Leave Tyler alone!!" he shouted.

For a moment, Ryan didn't know what Tyler was doing, but then he realized it. "What are you doing?!" Ryan shouted, "Stop!! Go home!!" Tyler attempted to push his younger brother away once more.

Tyler ignored Ryan's pleas, staring at Zander with a determined look in his eyes. "Zander, leave Tyler alone!! He didn't do anything!!" Ryan knew now what he was doing. He was trying to confuse Zander.

"What are you talking about?! Tylor, leavel Nowl!" Ryan tried to push his brother away. He looked at Zander. "Zander," Ryan shouted, "I stand by my proposition!"

Zander said nothing; he watched as the two argued amongst themselves. He closed his eyes and listened to the continuous shouts coming from the two. "Zander!!" He heard one of them shout. "Leave my brother alone!!" The grey-haired man looked at the one who had said that. Zander attempted to figure out who it was but failed. He turned to look at his men. "Shoot one of them; we'll take the other."

Ryan was still fighting with his brother, each of the two telling the other to leave. He heard a shot ring out, and his mind went blank.

Everything happened so fast.

Ryan was pushed out of the way, most likely by his brother. He saw red. He felt something warm trickle down his face and splash onto his shirt. Ryan looked up and saw his brother standing before him. He saw blood drip onto his pant leg. *Blood...?!* Ryan's head zipped up, following the trail of blood coming from his brother. "T-Tyler...?" He whispered.

There was a large stain of blood on his brother's chest. It was growing larger and larger by the minute. "Tyler!!" Ryan stood up quickly. He grabbed his brother and slowly kneeled down as Tyler let his full weight rest on his brother.

Ryan touched his brother's chest, feeling the blood flow through the thin material, staining his hands. "T-Tyler..." He heard his brother's breath grow slow. "Tyler, come on... Look at me, okay? Don't sleep... don't sleep..." Ryan rested his head on Tyler's shoulder.

"Excuse me," he heard Zander say, "Give us the body." Ryan was tapped on his shoulder. "You can go free."

Ryan felt tears threatening to overflow from his eyes. "R-Ryan..." He heard Tyler whisper. "This is like w-when we were k-kids, r-remember?" Ryan lifted his head and looked at the smile on Tyler's face. "You be me, and I'll be you..." Tyler touched the place where Ryan's heart was with his index finger. "Y-you be Tyler."

Tyler let out his final breath and the finger touching Ryan's heart fell to the ground.

"T-Tyler…" Ryan touched his brother's cheek. It was cold, as if his spirit had left just then. He looked at Tyler's eyes; the colour had left them and the veins had become a bright red. It was then Ryan realized he was holding his brother's corpse. Those tears he had tried to stop fell onto Tyler's face.

Ryan wiped the fallen tears from his brother's face. "Will you be able to revive him?" He asked, turning to the scientist.

Zander shrugged. "Who knows? We just got lucky with you." He looked at the corpse of the older brother. "We might bo ablo to," he smirked. "I just need more time."

Once Zander's men had loaded Tyler's corpse into the van, Ryan was approached by the tallest of the three men. "Go home," he said, "Before he changes his mind."

||++++++++++||

Ryan got off the motorcycle, parked it, and walked inside the cabin. There were no lights on; he assumed Royce was asleep. He set the keys down on a small table next to the front door. His feet were like jelly. He couldn't stand for more than a few seconds before stumbling. Ryan could still feel the rumble of the motorcycle running up and down his body.

His hair fell, covering his eyes, as he walked to the triangular table. Ryan sat down, sighing. He stared at the plastic bonsai plant that served at the centre piece. The room was silent, other than his shaky breathing. Ryan felt warm liquid trickle down his face and watched it hit the table.

His composure fell. Ryan held his head in his hands, sobbing loudly. He began to shout incoherently between the sobs. A string of curses flew out of his mouth; the filter that connected his mind and mouth faulty at the moment.

Ryan heard the pitter-patter of footsteps behind him. The soft touch of a hand caused him to turn around to face the person who had touched him. "Royce…" he said, shakily. "I'm sorry… Did I wake you up?"

There was a worried expression on her face. Her eyes were wide and her mouth agape. "Y-you've got blood on your shirt, Ryan," Royce said. She glanced around the room, confused. "Where's Tyler?" When she received no answer, she asked again but more stern. "Ryan." He looked at her, the redness from crying still evident. "Where's Tyler? Where's your brother?"

Ryan felt the tears fall once more. "T-Tyler…"

Royce laced their fingers together. "Ryan…? What happened?"

"T-Tyler's… Tyler is…" Ryan held Royce's hand tightly. "Zander -- he shot him, he shot him…" Ryan gripped her hand until his knuckles turned white. "He shot him!! Because of Zander, Tyler's dead!!" Royce had a worried look on her face as she watched him shout and cry. "Even after that, he still wanted his corpse!!"

Ryan buried his head in the crevices of his arms. He shouted again but more shrill. "I just led my own brother to his death!!" His voice became quiet, sobs still noticeable though soft. "H-he died, Royce… Wh-what am I supposed to do…?"

She ran her fingers through his hair. "You're twins, aren't you? You could easily be his proxy."

Ryan covered his mouth with his hand. "H-his blood…" he mumbled, "I can s-smell his b-blood.." He shot up from his chair and ran to the garbage bin by the fridge. Ryan threw up the fluids in his stomach. The bile that stuck to his lips was a mixture of green and red. He spewed into the bin violently, groaning for a few seconds before vomiting once more.

Ryan was on his knees after the sickness subsided. Strands of saliva were dripping down his chin as he groaned in pain. Tears were clouding his vision. Royce walked over to him, kneeling down next to him. She rubbed his head as he groaned some more.

Ryan leaned into the touch, yearning for comfort. He felt empty. His brother was gone. Ryan's reason for any of this was gone. The rough feeling of tissue snapped him out of his thoughts. His eyes moved to look at Royce. With a blank expression, she was wiping the excess fluids off his face.

He now noticed how numb his body felt. The comfort of a person's touch was null. He could barely feel the tissue repeatedly touching his cheek. His hand blindly wandered to touch Royce's face. He took note of how hot her cheek was. A pained smile appeared on his face. "Am I dead again, Royce?" he rasped out.

She shook her head. "You're not dead, Godfrey. Not fully."

"... So, this is how Tyler felt when he thought I died?" Ryan didn't wait for an answer from her. "Half of me is dead, you say?" He chuckled loudly. "When was I even alive in the first place...? I should've stayed a corpse..." He could see Royce's uncomfortable expression when he glanced to the left. "Royce..."

Her head perked up. "... Yes?"

"Tyler told me to be him and he'd be me."

She nodded, understanding.

"This means I have to go back home to resume playing my brother's life. I have to pick up where he left off..."

Royce nodded once more.

"Will you come with me...?" He asked quietly.

"... Come home with you?"

"Yeah." He took the tissue from her hand, throwing it behind him. "If I'm going to take up Tyler's role in the world, I want to be next to someone I can trust with all of this." Ryan laced their fingers together. "I want someone other than the people of Nico Global to know who I really am. I want you to be there. I want you to know me as Ryan. Not 'Tyler' and not 'Séan'."

Epilogue
////-----------------------------////

Ryan walked through the yard of the now familiar college campus. A few people greeted him as he walked around. Ryan simply smiled as he walked closer and closer to his destination. There were four red benches near the gates of the campus. Ryan walked over to a bench and sat down, pulling out a small notebook. About three minutes had passed before he felt a light tap on his shoulder. He turned around and saw Royce standing there. "Sup', Ryan." she said, chuckling.

He uttered a small smile. "Heya, Royce." Royce sat down next to him, placing her head on his shoulder. She watched him scribble away in the notebook. "Godfrey!" she whined, hugging his arm. "Pay attention to me!"

Ryan laughed and set the notebook down. He turned towards the girl and kissed her forehead. "I'm sorry for not paying attention to you, Royce. I'll bring you to the house later so we can eat something nice."

She smiled and continued to rub her head against his shoulder. Ryan didn't pick the notebook back up. He rested his head on Royce's and shut his eyes. Ryan sighed loudly and began to hum a random tune. He heard footsteps grow closer and closer. When he opened his eyes, he saw Felix. "Sorry to disturb you," he said, "I did what you asked."

Ryan got up from the bench and walked over to the blonde with a smile on his face. "You did? It's finished?"

Felix nodded. "Yeah, I had my sisters help clean it, if that's alright."

Ryan waved his hands. "No, no, no, it's fine. T-thank you, Felix."

"It's in the same place yours is. Just look under the flowers."

Ryan nodded and waved Royce and Felix good-bye. He walked to the car his parents bought him a few months ago. Opening the driver door, he sat down and started the car. Ryan entered the desired address into the GPS and began to drive.

He had asked Felix to do this after Tyler died. Through the file of information Royce had given him a while back, Ryan discovered Felix's aunt made a business of carving tombstones.

It was a grave for Tyler.

When he arrived at the very cemetery he was supposedly buried in, Ryan got out of the car and walked to the grave his family had made him when he died. There were three small pots covered in dirt underneath the large stone tablet that had Ryan's name on it. In each of the pots were three white roses.

Ryan carefully moved them so he could clearly see the marker he had requested. He smiled as he read what was etched into the stone.

Tyler Erin Godfrey
2000 - 2017
Son, brother, friend

He had asked Felix to put a specific quote at the bottom of the epitaph.

Proof the deceased will never stay deceased

Ryan smiled and tapped the stone with his index finger. "I love you, Ty." He went back to his car, and leaned against the driver's door. He didn't want to leave. Ryan imagined this being how Tyler felt when visiting him years ago.

People called him 'Tyler' now. His parents. His friends. Royce and Felix don't, though. Ryan chuckled, remembering when he got back home that night. Bryan and his mother had stayed awake, so they were still in the living room on the couch waiting for Tyler to return. When Ryan had returned back home, his mother was skeptical, but Bryan happily embraced him. It was a repeated string of 'thank God you're home' and 'don't ever do something like this again'.

His mother just stood by, waiting for Bryan to release him. When he did, she walked up to him slowly. She cupped his cheeks with her hands and chuckled. "Welcome home." she had said. Ryan certainly was happy to have his family back, but he would never see Tyler again.

This was fun. Playing Tyler. He missed his brother, so it wasn't hard to act like Tyler would. And, there were many times when Ryan could still hear the gunshot echoing through the air and see Tyler's blood dripping onto his fingers.

Ryan felt his phone vibrate in his pocket. He took it out and read the text notification from his mother. "How was school?" Ryan texted a reply and got into the car.

When he arrived home, Royce was sitting on the front porch reading something in a cream-coloured file folder. Ryan walked up to her, petting her hair. "Did you get a new client?" he asked, sitting down next to her. She simply nodded and continued to read the file intently.

After a few minutes, she set the file down and turned towards her boyfriend. "How was the thing Felix had made for you?"

Ryan smiled and chuckled lightly. "Perfect."

The teens stood up and entered the house. His parents weren't home, but the place still seemed loud. The amount of art and family pictures made the home seem more eccentric than normal. Ryan turned to Royce. "Would you like a drink?" he asked, gesturing to the kitchen.

She shook her head and pointed to the staircase to his bedroom. "You said you had almost finished it, right? I wanna see what you've got."

An uneasy look found its way onto Ryan's features. He nodded. "Don't laugh at me, Royce." He knew she meant well, but Royce had a habit of laughing at things that were meant to be sentimental.

"I won't, I won't, I promise." she said, seeming to fight the urge to smile.

Ryan led her to his bedroom and pulled a stack of canvases from his desk. She took the top of the stack and began to study it. "It looks nice." she said once finished. "Do you have a name for it yet?"

He shrugged. "I need something to fit the 'abstract' style of it all."

Royce nodded, thinking. "How 'bout something in Latin?"

Ryan shrugged again.

The light ring of a text echoed throughout the room. It was Ryan's phone. The text was from an unknown number. He unlocked his phone to take a look at the text. It simply said:

We've done it.

The number continued to send him pictures of documents that furthered Ryan's confusion. But then it happened.

Ryan was sent a picture of his brother.

Of *Tyler*.

He was alive.

How? *Why?*

The number sent another text.

Let's meet. We'll talk about this more in depth then.

Made in the USA
San Bernardino, CA
09 December 2019

61155205R00071